DELTORA QUEST 3

Shadowgate

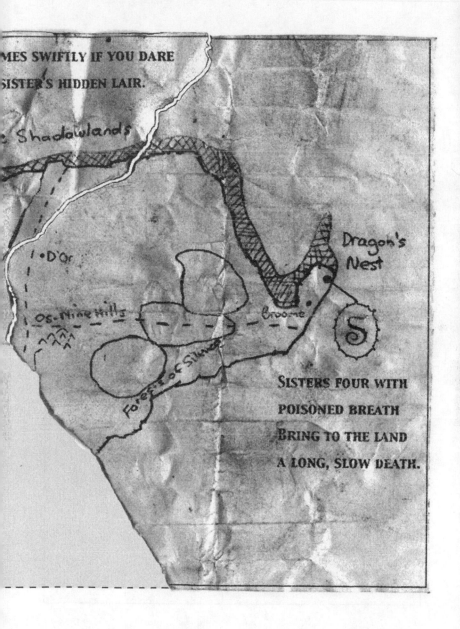

MES SWIFTLY IF YOU DARE
SISTER'S HIDDEN LAIR.

Shadowlands

Dragon's
Nest

• D'Or

Os-Nine Hills

Forest of Silver

Broome

S

SISTERS FOUR WITH
POISONED BREATH
BRING TO THE LAND
A LONG, SLOW DEATH.

DELTORA QUEST 3

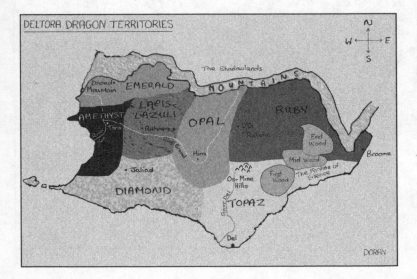

DELTORA QUEST 3

Shadowgate

Emily Rodda

A Scholastic Press book
from
Scholastic Australia

For Reuben Jakeman

LEXILE™ 630

Scholastic Press
345 Pacific Highway
Lindfield NSW 2070
an imprint of Scholastic Australia Pty Limited (ABN 11 000 614 577)
PO Box 579, Gosford NSW 2250.
www.scholastic.com.au

Part of the Scholastic Group
Sydney ● Auckland ● New York ● Toronto ● London ● Mexico City
● New Delhi ● Hong Kong ● Buenos Aires ● Puerto Rico

First published by Scholastic Australia in 2004.
Text and graphics copyright © Emily Rodda, 2004.
Graphics by Kate Rowe.
Cover illustrations copyright © Scholastic Australia, 2004.
Cover illustrations by Marc McBride.

Reprinted in 2004 (five times).

National Library of Australia Cataloguing-in-Publication entry
    Rodda, Emily, 1948–
    Shadowgate.
    For children aged 10 years and older.
    ISBN 1 86504 614 0.
    I. Title. (Series: Rodda, Emily, 1948– Deltora quest 3; 2)
A823.3.

Typeset in Palatino.

Printed by McPherson's Printing Group, Maryborough Vic.

10 9 8 7 6   4 5 6 7 / 0

CONTENTS

The story so far ...

Lief, Barda and Jasmine have begun a secret quest to find and destroy the Four Sisters, evil creations of the Shadow Lord which are poisoning Deltora. To succeed, they must wake Deltora's last seven dragons, which have been deep in enchanted sleep for centuries.

Deltora's dragons were hunted almost to extinction by the Shadow Lord's creatures, the seven Ak-baba. At last, only one dragon from each gem territory remained. To save them, Deltora's most famous explorer, Doran the Dragonlover (known to the dragons as Dragonfriend), persuaded the seven to sleep until a king, wearing the magic Belt of Deltora, called them to wake. He made each dragon swear that it would not take advantage of another's sleep to invade its territory.

The disappearance of the dragons allowed the Shadow Lord to put the Four Sisters in place. Only when the power of a dragon joins with the power of the gems in the Belt of Deltora, can the Sisters be destroyed.

The dragon of the topaz has been woken. With the help of a fragment of an ancient map and the dragon of the ruby, the companions have found and destroyed the Sister of the East, in Dragon's Nest, near the coastal city of Broome.

In doing so, they found another map fragment, telling them that the second Sister is hidden in the far north, at a place called Shadowgate.

Now read on ...

1 - Warning

The people of Broome were dancing. The music was loud. The floorboards of the great hall shook beneath the pounding of hundreds of feet.

Outside, it was dark. Cold wind moaned around the city walls, and waves crashed on the shore. But inside the great hall, all was warmth and light.

The people had much to celebrate.

King Lief, with his companions, Jasmine and Barda, had been in Broome for ten full days. That was a joy in itself. But there was something even better. During their stay, like a miracle, the barren land and the empty sea had come alive.

The fishing boats had begun hauling in fat fish. The hunters were bringing home meat almost every day. The crops were at last showing strong, new shoots.

Suddenly the long time of hunger was over. There was new life everywhere. It was even said that a scarlet dragon had been sighted in the sea above Dragon's Nest!

The people of Broome did not know how or why this wonder had occurred. They simply rejoiced. And their rejoicing was at its height on this, the last night of their young king's visit.

Part of a spinning circle of dancers in the centre of the hall, Lief looked as carefree as all the rest. But, in truth, his mind was on other things.

Only he, Barda, Jasmine and their friend Lindal knew that the land was healing because the evil thing called the Sister of the East had been destroyed.

Only they knew that the journey the companions would begin at dawn was to end in Shadowgate. There the Sister of the North lay hidden, spreading its poison and singing its song of death and despair.

The music ended with a mighty clash of cymbals. At the same moment, Lief caught sight of Jasmine beckoning urgently from the door. Filli was perched on her shoulder, almost hidden by her tangled black hair.

Lief hurried towards them.

'We went out to get some air,' Jasmine whispered as he reached her. 'See what we found!'

They slipped outside. Perched on the veranda rail outside the hall, golden eyes gleaming in the light of a hanging lantern, were two black birds.

Lief stared, startled. One of the birds was Kree, who was never far from Jasmine's side. But the other . . .

'Ebony!' he muttered.

Ebony was the most trusted of all the messenger

birds Jasmine had trained. On their second day in Broome, Ebony had arrived with a message from Doom, demanding news. She had flown back to Del bearing tidings as glad as Doom could wish.

Why had she returned so soon?

Jasmine held out the parchment she had taken from Ebony's leg. Lief recognised Doom's writing at once.

HIDDEN FLOCKS
TRAVEL SINGING.

SPARROW FRIENDS
FEATHER OLD NESTS ONLY DUCKS
TRUST CAGES.

BEAKS STOPPED CHIRPING BE TO
CHICKS ARE YOU TWITTERING
WHISPERS WINGS ARE THERE.

YET AS TREES KNOWN MORE
BRANCHES NOTHING HOOTS.
HERE FLUTTERING THINGS WITH
EGGS REAL PECKING WILL I FLY.
SEED FORTUNE PERCHES GOOD EAGLE.

'Doom has gone mad,' said Jasmine. 'Or . . . is he trying to write poetry? If so, he has no talent for it. This does not even rhyme.'

Lief grinned at the thought of Doom as a poet. 'Poems do not have to rhyme,' he said. 'But they do have to make a kind of sense. Doom has used a new code.'

'Well, I cannot make head nor tail of it,' Jasmine

said flatly. 'It seems just a lot of nonsense about birds.'

Lief frowned over the note. 'Perhaps it is a warning to us to keep Kree safe,' he muttered. 'Doom thinks someone drugged Kree's water, the night he returned to Del. And he must be right. Kree remembers nothing of that night, or the following day.'

'I do not need a warning,' Jasmine snapped. 'I do not need a drawing of birds being freed to remind me how lucky Kree was to escape death.'

An idea flashed into Lief's mind. He scanned the message rapidly.

'Why, of course!' he exclaimed. 'The picture is the clue. We must free the birds!'

He took the stub of a pencil from his pocket and crossed out some of the words in the message.

'You see?' he said. 'That is what the picture means. All the words that have anything to do with birds— "flocks", "singing", "sparrow" and so on—have to be taken out of the message before it can be read.'

Jasmine began reading the new note. '"Hidden ... travel. Friends ... old ... only ... trust ..."—it still does not make sense!'

Then she saw the second small trick, and smiled. 'Unless you read each sentence backwards!' she added.

Lief could not return her smile. Grimly he spoke the words of the message aloud.

'"Travel hidden. Trust only old friends. There are whispers you are to be stopped. Nothing more known as yet. I will deal with things here. Good fortune."'

Jasmine did not spend time wondering what had made her father send such a message. She concentrated on practical matters.

'It will not be easy to travel hidden,' she said. 'Everyone knows we are touring the kingdom. Everywhere people will be watching, in case we come their way.'

'Indeed.' Lief was still staring at Doom's note. 'And the guardian of the Sister of the North among them, it seems. The Shadow Lord must have sensed that the Sister of the East is no more. He cannot know if we found the map fragment directing us to Shadowgate. But he is taking no chances.'

Jasmine slowly nodded agreement. 'And plainly the guardian of the north has allies,' she said. 'Doom has heard rumours ... surely there could *be* no rumours if only one person was involved.'

Lief looked down at the magic Belt of Deltora. The seven great gems gleamed, the topaz and the ruby brighter than all the rest.

The Belt's power keeps the Shadow Lord back for now, but his hand still stretches into Deltora, he thought bitterly. We cannot trust smiling faces or loyal words. Even here in Broome . . .

He felt a small, strong hand grip his own. He lifted his head and met Jasmine's bright eyes.

'I doubt we have an enemy in Broome, but we will take no risks,' she said, as though she had read his mind. 'We will leave here now—tonight. Then . . . we will disappear. We will disguise ourselves and take new names. We have done that before. Remember?'

'Yes,' Lief muttered. 'But I did not think we would ever have to do it again. In those days, I was not king and the Belt of Deltora had not been restored. In those days, I thought that if we succeeded in our quest we would all live happily ever after. I did not dream the nightmare would go on, and on—'

He and Jasmine spun around as the door to the hall swung open in a blast of sound. Barda and Lindal of Broome strode out onto the veranda.

'Lindal saw you through the window,' Barda said. 'What—?'

He broke off as his eyes fell on the parchment in Lief's hand. His face sobered, and he glanced at Lindal.

'You will be wanting privacy,' Lindal said quickly.

She turned to go back into the hall.

Trust only old friends.

'No, Lindal, please stay,' begged Lief. 'We need your help.'

✻

Less than an hour later, four figures slipped silently out of the city gates. The dance was still in full swing, and no-one saw them go.

Even if they had been seen, it was unlikely that the first three would have been recognised.

Only the woman turning to close the gates behind them would have been familiar. Lindal looked as she always did—tall and straight in leather jacket, leggings and boots, her shaved skull painted with swirling red patterns.

Her friends, however, now looked very different.

All were dressed in the drab, close-fitting woollen caps and long oiled coats of Broome fisher folk, and their most famous features had been disguised.

Lief no longer wore his cloak, and the Belt of Deltora was concealed beneath his clothes. Jasmine's hair was hidden under her cap and her face was streaked with grime so that she looked like a grubby young boy. Barda's dark beard had been cut back to rough stubble.

'It was bad enough playing the part of a beggar, in the old days,' he grumbled. 'But at least I still had my beard then. And I did not stink of fish that died before I was born!'

Lindal laughed. 'Your garments smell very strong,

I must admit. I suspect that no-one will want to keep company with the rough-looking man Berry, and his two young nephews, Lewin and Jay, for long.'

'That will suit Berry, Lewin and Jay very well,' Jasmine answered, though Filli, crouched on her shoulder and rubbing his nose, plainly disagreed.

'Filli will have to stay hidden, Jasmine,' Lindal warned. 'And Kree will have to keep his distance.'

'I know,' sighed Jasmine, glancing at the black bird perched on her arm. 'And the journey to Shadowgate will be very long. I only wish Honey, Bella and Swift were still with us.'

'The horses are back in Del by now, no doubt,' said Barda. 'But we may be able to buy others in the north.'

Lindal shook her head in wonder. Horses were unknown in Broome, where people used their own legs to carry them from place to place, whatever the distance.

'Thank you for all you have done for us, Lindal,' Lief said, anxious to be gone. 'Send Ebony back to Del in the morning. And remember, the ruby dragon has promised me that it will do the people of Broome no harm—as long as they leave it in peace.'

'Time will tell,' Lindal said darkly. 'I do not place great value on a dragon's promise. Perhaps the ruby beast kept faith with Doran the Dragonlover. But that does not mean it will keep faith with you.'

And at that very moment, Kree screeched a warning, and the stars above them were blotted out.

The ruby dragon swept above them. Its red scales

glittered in the moonlight. Its wingbeats were louder than the wind.

'Why, the beast has already broken its vow!' cried Lindal furiously, reaching for a spear. 'It thinks to take advantage of the celebration, to plunder the city!'

'Wait!' shouted Lief, throwing himself in front of her. 'Lindal! Let me speak to it!'

Lindal tightened her lips, but pointed her spear to the ground.

The dragon landed in front of them and settled itself comfortably.

'Greetings, king of Deltora,' it said to Lief. 'You are leaving Broome a little earlier than you planned.'

'Yes,' Lief said uncomfortably. 'It became . . . necessary.'

The dragon nodded. 'I approve,' it said. 'In darkness, we can fly unseen.'

'*What?*' exclaimed Barda.

The dragon turned its flat, red eyes in his direction. 'Sadly, I cannot take you all the way to the second Sister,' it said. 'My oath to Dragonfriend prevents me crossing my border. But I will take you as far as I am able.'

It bared its terrible fangs in what it no doubt intended as a smile.

'Do you like my surprise?' it asked. 'Are you not pleased? Dragonfriend always said it was the greatest happiness, to ride upon a dragon.'

2 - North

It was like hurtling through a tunnel of darkness. Below them, the lights of villages flashed into view and disappeared again. Above them gleamed the silent stars. But where the ruby dragon flew, there was only blackness, and cold, and the sound of the wind.

Bound with ropes to the dragon's neck, the companions felt as battered as shellfish clinging to the wave-beaten rocks of Dragon's Nest. Kree and Filli huddled motionless beneath Jasmine's jacket, making not a sound.

They had flown for hours. Lief had lost all track of time. Then, suddenly, his stomach gave a sickening lurch.

They were falling. They were plummeting down, down, and the thick blackness of the land was rising to meet them.

Lief screwed his streaming eyes shut.

Abruptly, the downward plunge ceased. The roaring of the wind died. Now there was only a slow, rhythmic sound—the sound of the dragon's wings, steadily beating.

Slowly, Lief opened his eyes.

They were hovering just above a field which was bordered by a massive hedge. On three sides the hedge was studded with white flowers that fluttered in the breeze. The remaining side was dark.

Beyond this dark side was a forest. Behind the trees towered the great mountains of Deltora's northern border, snow glimmering on their peaks.

The dragon sank to earth and folded its wings.

'This is the place where I must leave you,' it said. 'I feel it.'

The ropes loosened as Barda cut through the knots. Lief slid down onto the ground and sprawled there, trying to gather his wits. The earth was rough, and the patchy grass was mingled with some sort of herb that smelled unpleasantly like over-ripe fruit.

'Ah, it is freezing, and as dark as pitch!' he heard Barda say.

There was the sound of scraping flint. Light began dancing on the grass as a lantern flamed into life.

Lief crawled to his knees, feeling as stiff as an old, old man and as weak as a baby. He was ashamed to see Jasmine already standing up, with Kree perched on her arm and Filli chattering on her shoulder.

'Where are we, dragon?' Jasmine was asking. 'Can

you show us on our map?'

'I know nothing of maps,' the dragon said. 'I know only that this is the far north of my territory, and very near to the land of the opal.'

It turned its great head towards the forest. 'As I landed I saw lights there, and heard music,' it added helpfully. 'Humans are camped not far away. No doubt they can tell you what you wish to know.'

Lief found his voice. 'Thank you for carrying us,' he said. 'You have saved us weeks of travelling.'

The dragon bowed. 'It is the least I could do for the king who roused me to life again,' it said, its red eyes gleaming. 'Dreams are all very fine, but not as fine as the splash of sparkling water, or the warmth of the sun.'

The breeze blew, bringing with it the over-sweet, slightly rotten smell of the field, and the faint sound of music. The dragon moved restlessly.

'I must go,' it murmured. 'I do not like the smell of this place. I know that our tie will not be broken now, wherever you may go, but partings make me sad. Farewell. I will think of you.'

Without waiting for an answer, it launched itself into the air. In moments it was gone.

Barda looked around. 'It would be best to stay away from the forest for tonight, I think,' he said. 'Let us see what is behind the hedge on the other side.'

They shouldered their packs and walked across the field. When they reached the hedge, they received their first surprise. It was not covered with flowers at all, but with huge, white moths.

The moths were big as small birds, and all exactly alike. There were thousands of them. A few were on the outer leaves of the hedge. Most were clinging to twigs deep inside it. All were slowly opening and closing their wings, which bore odd red markings.

'There is something strange about them,' Jasmine said, peering at them. 'They hardly look real!'

Impulsively, Lief stretched out a finger and gently touched the tip of a moth's wing.

At once, the red markings lit up like tiny beacons.

Exclaiming in shock, Lief jumped back. The next instant the moth spat—a thin jet of liquid that sizzled as it hit the ground.

Filli squealed. Kree screeched and took flight.

'Lief, you fool!' Barda thundered. 'Did it hit you?'

'No,' gasped Lief, very shaken. 'But it was a near thing!'

'Beware!' Jasmine said urgently. 'Get back!'

All the moths around the first one were now lighting up and spitting their poison. The hedge blazed with tiny red lights. But none of the creatures moved from their places, and after a few moments the spitting stopped, and the red markings began to fade.

'What *are* these creatures?' Jasmine cried, as Kree landed on her arm once more, very ruffled. 'It is as if they are alive, yet not alive. As if—'

Lief gasped. He had suddenly seen something astounding.

The strange red markings on the moths' wings made words.

'The moths make a warning line!' he exclaimed. He moved a little closer to one of the moths and, being careful not to touch it, pointed to the letters one by one.

'Keep Out,' Jasmine said. 'So it is forbidden to pass through this hedge. But who has forbidden it? And why? What is on the other side?'

'I do not give a fig!' Barda growled irritably. 'There seem to be no moths in the hedge on the forest side of the field. Come on!'

They trudged wearily to the other side of the field. They found that the dark hedge was thin and full of gaps. Plainly people had been pushing through it very recently, moving in and out of the field.

Jasmine lifted her arm to place Kree on her shoulder. As she settled him there, her hand brushed the back of his neck, and he squawked. Puzzled, she lifted her hand to the light. It was streaked with blood.

She clicked her tongue in annoyance, pulled Kree

to her and examined his neck. He clucked uneasily.

'The Orchard Keeper's beak must have jabbed you here, Kree,' she murmured, dabbing his neck with creamy green ointment from the small jar she carried with her everywhere. 'I had not noticed. It is a small wound, but deep. No doubt it pulled open when you were startled just now. We must—'

Abruptly she broke off, listening intently.

'What is it?' Lief hissed.

'Someone is coming,' Jasmine breathed.

Instantly Barda blew out the lantern. They pressed into the hedge, and peered through the sparse leaves.

As their eyes adjusted to the darkness, they saw that the hedge was separated from the forest by a deep, gaping ditch. They could see little else.

Kree squawked softly.

'Go, then,' Jasmine whispered reluctantly.

Kree hopped out of the hedge, flew over the ditch and disappeared into the darkness.

In breathless silence, they waited. In a few moments Lief and Barda heard what Jasmine's sharper ears had heard before them—the cracking of twigs, the thudding of feet, a stream of grunts and panted curses.

Kree screeched from the trees.

'An enemy,' Jasmine breathed. 'Kree is sure of that. But there is something he does not—'

She fell silent as the bobbing, flickering light of a torch became visible through the trees.

The sounds came closer. The torchlight grew

brighter. And suddenly a giant of a man burst through the last of the trees and stood at the edge of the ditch, breathing heavily.

He was vast, with legs like tree-trunks, a huge belly and enormous, beefy shoulders. He held a club in one hand, and a flaming torch in the other. His massive arms were bare, and adorned with beaten metal bands. Every one of his sausage-like fingers shone with rings. Animal skins, lashed in place by leather cords, covered his body.

And then he lifted the torch and they saw his face.

They saw tiny, fierce eyes blazing over a snuffling, fleshy snout. They saw ears flopping amid bristly brown hair. They saw a snarling mouth and razor sharp tusks.

The man had the head of a wild pig.

The pig-man growled ferociously, his small eyes darting left and right, searching the darkness.

'I know you are here, spies,' he roared. 'I heard your voices. I saw your light!'

There was a rustle in the tree above him and he looked up, snarling. But when he saw only a black bird, silently watching him, he grunted in disgust and looked down again.

'How did you cross the line, spies?' he roared. 'What trick did you use to break into the secret field? Are you going to tell me you fell out of the sky?'

Lief, Barda and Jasmine looked at one another, all realising the truth at the same moment. They had assumed that the moths in the hedge were to stop people moving from the field to whatever was on the other side.

But it had been the other way around. The moths were to keep intruders *out* of the field, and out of this part of the forest.

How could they have known? They really *had* dropped into the field from the sky. But they could not tell the pig-man that. And, even if they did, he plainly would not believe it.

'Show yourselves!' the pig-man bellowed.

The companions remained utterly still. There was a chance that if they remained hidden, he would grow tired of the dark and the cold and go back to his den.

Though together they could no doubt overpower him at last, none of them wanted to be forced to try. They still had far to go. Their quest was too important for them to risk needless injury. The pig-man was powerful and filled with fury.

But that is not all, Lief thought, his skin crawling as he stared at the ugly figure stamping on the other side of the ditch. There is malice here. Something terrible, that none of us understand.

He was shivering, as if chilled to the bone.

Evil was near, very near. He could feel it, coming closer. He could almost see it, rushing, shapeless, through the shadows of the ditch. He had an absurd urge to shout—to jump up and shriek a warning.

'You are hiding in the ditch, or behind the hedge!' bawled the pig-man. 'Come out, or I will come and get you!'

He waited a moment, then lumbered forward and

began sliding clumsily into the ditch. Mud squelched as his feet hit the bottom.

A black shadow soared past his head, and a beak snapped, just missing his ear. He staggered, slipped and pitched over, disappearing from sight.

'No, Kree!' breathed Jasmine, clenching her fists anxiously as Kree returned to the attack.

The pig-man crawled to his feet, cursing. He was wet and smeared with slimy filth, but the torch was still alight. Roaring with anger, he wallowed in the mud, swinging the torch above his head to keep off the swooping bird.

The torch flame blazed as it swung wildly from side to side. Light danced in the muddy ditch, banishing shadows where it fell. Suddenly, Kree gave a screech and seemed to stop dead in mid-air. Then he soared upwards, disappearing into the blackness of the sky.

The pig-man grunted with satisfaction, but as he lowered the torch he gave a slight start. He leaned over a little, pushing his hideous, bristly head forward to peer into the gloom further along the ditch.

Then he chuckled. 'Peek-a-boo, I see you!' he growled.

A chill ran down Lief's spine.

The pig-man raised his club, took a step forward . . .

Then he screamed—a shrill, terrified squeal that raised the hair on the back of Lief's neck. And out of the shadows of the ditch rose a thing of nightmare—a vast thing, black and hooded.

3 – The Masked Ones

The black thing loomed above the pig-man, darker than the night. He screamed again and staggered backwards. The thing did not move. Thin, white hands crept out of its billowing blackness—hands with long, grasping fingers that had no marks, no lines, no nails.

The fingers twitched. Then smoothly, impossibly, they began to lengthen, snaking forward to fasten around the pig-man's neck.

The next moment he was jerked off his feet, choking and gurgling, his boots kicking at the sides of the ditch, the torch still clutched in his hand.

The thing shook him, like a dog shaking a rat. The terrible gurgling sounds stopped abruptly, and the pig-man went limp.

The thing tossed him aside. His huge body sailed through the air like a floppy, broken doll and fell heavily into the mud. With a hiss the torch went out, and the ditch was plunged into darkness.

It had all happened in the blink of an eye. Shocked, not daring to move, Lief, Barda and Jasmine crouched in their hiding place. Then, high above them, Kree screeched.

'Kree says the thing has vanished,' Jasmine said in a low voice.

And Lief knew that it was so. He was no longer shivering. But cold dread still gripped him like icy, white fingers.

'It may return at any moment,' he muttered. 'We must get into the forest.'

In feverish haste, they pushed forward to the edge of the ditch. Kree flew down to them. He perched on Jasmine's shoulder and made a low sound.

'Kree saw the thing in the shadows before the pig-man did,' Jasmine said. 'That was why he flew away. He says the shadow thing was not alive. Not alive as we are.'

'It was alive enough to kill,' Barda said grimly.

The breeze was still blowing gently. The only sound was the rustling of the leaves.

Something nagged at the edge of Lief's mind, but he could not quite catch hold of it. His brain was telling him that something had changed. But he was too tired and shocked to think what it was.

Barda lit the lantern again, and the companions slid down into the ditch. It was very deep. Standing at the bottom was like being buried under the earth. Sound was muffled, and the air smelled of damp and slime.

The body of the pig-man lay nearby, face down in the mud. Jasmine darted over to it.

'Jasmine!' Barda hissed angrily.

Jasmine ignored him. She bent over the mud-smeared body for a long moment. Then, rapidly, she patted the animal skins that swathed it. Something rustled, and she drew out a bundle of green papers.

Barda lowered the lantern. By its glow they read the words on the paper at the top of the bundle.

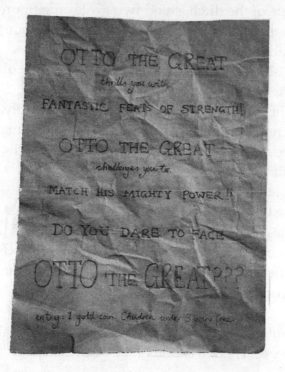

OTTO THE GREAT
thrills you with
FANTASTIC FEATS OF STRENGTH!

OTTO THE GREAT
challenges you to
MATCH HIS MIGHTY POWER!!

DO YOU DARE TO FACE

OTTO THE GREAT???

entry: 1 gold coin. Children under 5 years free.

Jasmine flicked through the other papers. They were all the same.

'So now we know his name, and how he earned his living,' she said. 'But how he died, I cannot tell. His neck does not seem to be broken. It is as though his heart just—stopped.'

Lief's scalp was crawling. 'Let us get away from here!' he said hoarsely.

'It is too late for that!' a sharp voice barked.

Very startled, Lief, Barda and Jasmine looked up.

And there, standing looking down at them from the edge of the ditch, stood two grotesque figures.

A man with the head of an eagle. A woman with the head of a fox.

And behind them was a crowd—a crowd of beings that were all half-human, half-beast.

The music has stopped! Lief thought wildly. *That* is what I noticed at the edge of the ditch. The pig-man must have come from the camp in the forest. They heard his screams. And now they think—

'*Madaras!*' cried the fox-woman shrilly.

Instantly all the animal people behind her leaped into the ditch. Kree took flight. Lief, Barda and Jasmine fell beneath the press of a dozen struggling bodies.

They fought valiantly. But against so many, they had no chance.

✳

In minutes, the companions were being dragged through the forest. Their weapons had been taken. Dozens of hands held them fast. Their captors jostled all around them, talking angrily in a strange language. The only words Lief could make out were two names—'Otto' and, repeated over and over again, 'Bess'.

'You are making a mistake!' Lief shouted. 'We did not kill Otto. He—'

'Save your lies, bareface spy!' snarled the eagle-man from behind him. 'You will rue the day you crossed the line of the Masked Ones.'

'The Masked Ones!' Lief heard Barda exclaim.

'Ah, yes! Pretend you did not know!' the eagle-man jeered.

Masks! Lief thought, with a shock. He looked around at his captors.

Their heads looked so real! But now he could see what should have been obvious to him all along.

These people were all wearing *masks*! Amazing masks, that covered their heads closely, fitting like a second skin.

'*Lat as kall tam na, Quill!*' growled a short woman with the head of a frog.

'*Na! Bess mast say tam,*' the eagle-man muttered.

Lights became visible through the trees, and moments later the companions were being dragged into a crowded clearing. A great fire blazed in the centre. There was the smell of cooking, and a confused roar of sound.

A huge banner had been stretched between two trees. It flapped lightly in the breeze.

23

Everywhere, masked people were shaking their fists, shouting and wailing. Lief glimpsed a wolf face, a rat face, the face of a ginger cat, and several bird heads.

A grinning, hairy mask with small black eyes twitched into view. It belonged to a ragged boy who had wormed his way through the legs of the crowd to stare at the prisoners.

The face was full of cunning. Lief knew that he had seen something like it before, but could not think where. He only knew that he distrusted it.

Among the trees that surrounded the clearing stood many wooden wagons. Washing lines strung with clothes sagged between them. Big grey horses with plaited manes gazed curiously at the shouting people.

Suddenly the crowd parted to reveal a wagon standing all by itself in a bright circle of light created by dozens of lanterns.

In front of the wagon, seated in an huge chair with gold-painted arms, was an enormous woman.

Somehow Lief knew that this was Bess.

She was vast—at least twice as large as the pig-man. Her billowing purple skirts were like silken tents. Her fringed, embroidered shawls were as large as bed sheets. Her great arms jangled with bracelets as big as the wheels of a small cart.

And her head was the head of a vast brown owl.

Lief only had time for a single, startled glance before he was thrown forward. He fell heavily, face down, in the dust at the owl-woman's feet. Jasmine and Barda thudded to the ground beside him.

'*Whar as Otto?*' he heard a deep voice demand hoarsely.

'*Otto as dad, Bess!*' Lief heard the fox-woman cry out. '*Tay kalled am!*'

Why, they are not really speaking a different language at all! Lief thought. 'It just *sounds* different. They use an 'a' sound in place of 'e', 'i' 'o' and 'u' in all words except names. And they use 't' instead of 'th'. The owl-woman said, 'Where is Otto?' The fox-woman answered, 'Otto is dead, Bess! They killed him!'

The stretcher bearing the lifeless body of the pig-man was carried into the circle of light. The panting bearers put the stretcher down and backed away.

Bess looked down at the body. Her great fists clenched.

'*Gat tam ap!*' she growled. '*Lat may say tayar aglay fasas!*' She drew a long, narrow knife from the silken folds of her skirt.

'Lief! She is going to cut our throats!' Barda muttered, as the crowd's noise rose. 'Tell her who you are. Show her the Belt. It is our only chance . . .'

His voice trailed off as he was hauled to his feet. At the same moment, Lief himself was jerked upward.

His legs would not hold him. Head bowed, he sagged between his captors.

Tell her who you are. Show her the Belt . . . It is our only chance.

Slowly, Lief looked up.

The owl-woman gasped, and her hand flew to her heart.

'*Bede!*' she shrieked. '*Bede, ma san!*' She threw the knife aside and began struggling to rise from her chair.

Dead silence had fallen in the clearing. Lief stood gaping. What had she said?

Bede, my son!

Tears pouring from her eyes, Bess held out her arms to him.

Someone pushed him from behind and he stumbled forward. The owl-woman seized him. Suddenly he was being crushed in her powerful arms, pressed to her heaving chest.

Gold bracelets dug hard into his spine. He was suffocating in a tangle of silken shawls that smelled strongly of spices, smoke and over-ripe fruit. In panic he struggled to free himself, but the mighty arms clasping him were like steel bands.

'*Bess!*' The harsh voice of the eagle-man seemed to

26

be coming from far away. *'Stap! Ha as nat Bede! Ha cannat ba Bede!'*

Lief felt the huge arms quiver. Then, slowly, they began to loosen. Gasping for breath, he threw himself backwards, and tumbled to the ground.

When at last he looked up, Bess was lying back in her chair, panting. Her eyes were closed. The eagle-man stood beside her, his hand on her shoulder.

'Confess!' he shouted at Lief, Barda and Jasmine. 'Confess to our leader that you have been sent here to spy upon us and destroy us! Confess that you are servants of the evil tyrant, King Lief of Del!'

Lief's heart lurched.

'We are travellers from Broome!' Jasmine's clear voice cried out. 'My uncle's name is Berry. My brother and I are Lewin and Jay. We have done nothing wrong!'

'Lies!' the eagle-man roared. 'You broke into our secret field. Then you killed the one who went to find you. We caught you in the act!'

'No!' shouted Jasmine. 'A thing of darkness killed your friend. We saw it!'

The eagle-man laughed scornfully.

Bess's eyes opened. But she did not look at the eagle-man, or at Jasmine. Instead, she looked at Lief.

'Is this true?' she asked, almost gently.

Lief met her gaze squarely. He knew that he had to make the most of her softened mood. He had to convince her.

'It is true,' he said. 'The thing was hiding in the

ditch. It caught hold of Otto around the neck, and he died. We did not harm him, I swear it!'

'*Ha lays, Bess!*' hissed the eagle-man. '*Tay ar spays!*'

'We are *not* spies!' Lief exclaimed furiously, without thinking.

There was a murmur in the crowd. The eagle-man drew back with a hiss.

'Then how do you know our tongue, bareface?' he spat.

Cursing himself for his foolishness, Lief spoke directly to Bess, forcing himself to keep his voice level.

'I used my ears,' he said. 'Your tongue sounded strange to me at first, but soon I found I could understand it.'

And perhaps the great topaz I wear beneath my clothes helped me, he added to himself. The topaz that sharpens the mind. The topaz that has been so powerful ever since the golden dragon came back to life.

But Bess had leaned forward, her eyes shining.

'Of course!' she breathed. 'It comes naturally to you. Now I see—'

She broke off, and shook her head. '*Ay mast nat bay hastay,*' she murmured to herself. '*Ay mast bay shar . . .*'

She raised her voice. 'Lock them in Otto's wagon,' she ordered, gesturing at the prisoners. 'I will examine his body. Then I will decide what is to be done.'

4 - A Surprising Offer

T he companions were thrown into a nearby wagon, locked in, and left in thick darkness which smelled strongly of sweat and damp fur. As soon as their captors' footsteps had died away, there was a cautious squawk from outside. Keeping out of sight, Kree had followed them.

'He says they took the key,' Jasmine whispered. 'He cannot help us.'

Quickly they began feeling around, looking for a weapon, or a way of escape. They found nothing but a wooden trunk full of animal skins and a mattress covered with a stinking fur rug. They could discover no gaps or loose boards anywhere.

At last they gave up. None of them felt like sitting on the mattress. They sat on the floor, resting their backs against the wall.

'Bess may well decide that we are innocent,' said

Jasmine, stroking Filli to comfort him. 'She wants Lief, at least, to live.'

Lief squirmed, remembering Bess's crushing embrace.

'Bess may want us to live, but that fellow in the eagle mask is thirsting for our blood,' Barda said.

'If they knew who we really are, things would be even worse,' Lief muttered. 'It sounded as if they would be only too glad to kill Lief the tyrant.'

He had tried to keep his voice level, but the bitterness he felt as he said the last words was very clear.

'They must be mad to call you a tyrant!' Jasmine exclaimed. 'Or ... perhaps they are allies of the guardian of the north! Clearly they are sorcerers. The moths prove that—and so does the thing in the ditch.'

'The thing in the ditch killed one of their own people,' said Barda, shaking his head. 'It cannot have been their creature. Besides, nothing I know of the Masked Ones leads me to think they would serve the Shadow Lord—or anyone else.'

'What do you know?' asked Lief.

'Only what I have heard from travellers,' Barda said. 'Masked Ones have been roaming the far-flung parts of Deltora for centuries. They are entertainers—acrobats and singers and such. The troupe is like a large family. It keeps to itself, passing its secrets on from generation to generation—'

Outside, Kree screeched warningly.

'They are coming back,' Jasmine whispered.

Hastily, the three scrambled to their feet.

A key turned in the lock. The door of the wagon creaked open. The shape of the fox-woman loomed in the gap.

'There are no marks upon Otto's body, except what seem to be burns around the neck,' the fox-woman snapped. 'Therefore, Bess has chosen to believe your story. She wishes to see you.'

✳

A small round table draped with a purple cloth had been placed in front of Bess's chair, and three stools had been set out for Lief, Barda and Jasmine. In moments they found themselves drinking vegetable soup, eating strips of warm, flat bread, and being treated as honoured guests.

The fox-woman, whose name was Rust, stood behind Bess's chair, her sharp eyes watching everything they did. Otto's body had been removed. The eagle-man was nowhere to be seen.

All the other Masked Ones had gone back to dancing and playing music. But Lief saw them staring curiously at the companions whenever they thought they could do so without being noticed.

'They keep their masks on even when they eat!' Jasmine whispered in Lief's ear.

And it was true. Even the children ate, drank and played with their masks firmly in place. It was fascinating, yet it made Lief uneasy. With faces so well hidden, it was impossible to tell what people were thinking. Only the eyes and hands provided clues.

Now that he was calmer, he could see that some of the masks were better than others. The frog-woman's mask, for example, was a glistening green masterpiece. Rust's fox mask, too, and Bess's owl's head, looked so real that it was hard to believe they had been made by human hands.

But many of the masks worn by others in the troupe were far more ordinary. They were just false heads of fur or feathers with holes for eyes, mouth and nose.

Bess was gobbling her food, filling her vast soup bowl again and again from a pot simmering on a fire beside her. She seemed tense, as if with excitement.

'What has brought you to this part of the country, may I ask?' she said abruptly, at last.

'My nephews and I left Broome to find work,' Barda said, telling their planned story. 'Food is scarce at home.'

'It is the same everywhere,' Bess nodded. 'But, just lately, things have begun growing again! That is why we came to this place, which we have not visited for many years. We have been here five days, for we were delighted to find that—'

She broke off as Rust's hand tightened on her shoulder.

Lief wondered what she had been going to say. Plainly, it was something that Rust did not think the visitors should know. Something about why the Masked Ones were camped in the forest.

And why *are* they here? he thought suddenly. There

is no space in the forest for staging a performance. And clearly they want people to stay *out* of the field.

He met the fox-woman's suspicious eyes.

She, at least, thinks Bess is wrong to trust us, he thought. She thinks we are lying. And she is right, of course. We will have to be very careful.

He concentrated on keeping his face expressionless, wishing heartily that he had a mask himself.

Bess cleared her throat. 'Tomorrow we will be moving west along the mountains, to a place called Happy Vale,' she said. 'See here!'

She pulled a pink leaflet from the folds of her skirt and held it out to Barda.

THE MASKED ONES!

☆ Jugglers ☆ Acrobats ☆ Magic
☆ Fortune-telling ☆ Mind reading
☆ Games of skill ☆ Feats of strength
☆ Prizes to be won!!

COME ONE, COME ALL!

You Will Not Believe Your Eyes!

NEXT PERFORMANCE HAPPY VALE

'We have not performed in Happy Vale for a long time,' said Bess, watching intently as Lief, Barda and Jasmine read the notice. 'It will be a grand night. And it could be just the first of many grand nights for you. If you accept my offer.'

The companions looked up at her in surprise.

Bess leaned forward. 'You are looking for work,' she said. 'Well, I am offering you not only work, but a home as well. I am inviting you to join us—to join the Masked Ones!'

Stunned, Barda glanced at Lief and Jasmine, then turned back to Bess.

'We are most honoured,' he said carefully. 'But the Masked Ones are entertainers—fine ones, too, I hear. We are only humble fishermen.'

'Ah! But we can train you for greater things,' cried Bess eagerly. 'Many here were not born Masked Ones.'

She nodded as Barda looked surprised. 'It has always been our habit to adopt bareface infants and small children—orphans, with no family to care for them,' she said. 'But a year or two ago, I began taking in older children—and adults as well.'

The fox-woman sniffed disapprovingly.

'It was necessary if the troupe was to survive,' Bess said, raising her voice slightly. 'Our old families have dwindled sadly. So—will you join us, Berry? If you do, you will be set for life! The Masked Ones look after their own.'

'Do not try to persuade them, Bess,' snapped Rust.

'Surely we have enough bareface hangers-on already!'

Bess's huge fists clenched. 'These would not be hangers-on!' she growled. 'Have you forgotten who we lost tonight?'

'We lost a friend and brother—one of the inner circle,' Rust said resentfully.

'We also lost our strong man,' said Bess. 'How can we perform at Happy Vale or anywhere else without one of our most popular acts? Otto would have been the first to say it is impossible!'

She pointed at Barda. 'Look at this fellow! Powerful as an ox! Dressed for the part, he would make an excellent strong man.'

'And what of his nephews?' Rust enquired icily, turning her fox head to look at Lief and Jasmine. 'How will they earn their keep?'

'Oh, I am sure they can be trained for something,' Bess said, with false casualness. 'Lewin, for example, has the look of one who can sing like a bird.'

'Bess, you say that only because he reminds you of Bede!' Rust exploded. 'Think what you are doing!'

'How dare you question me?' thundered Bess. 'Leave us!'

Without a word, the fox-woman backed away and disappeared into the shadows.

'Truly, I am not sure that I would make a good singer, Bess,' Lief murmured. 'My voice is not—'

'Nonsense, Lewin!' Jasmine broke in, to his great surprise. 'Your voice is very sweet.'

While Lief was still gaping at her, she turned to Barda.

'I think we should accept this generous offer, Uncle,' she said firmly. 'After all, the Masked Ones are moving west, as we always intended to do. Why should we not join them—at least for a time? There is safety in numbers.'

Plainly, she was giving Lief and Barda a message. She was telling them that joining the Masked Ones would be the best possible disguise.

'Oh,' Barda said blankly. 'Well, perhaps . . . for a time . . .'

'Excellent!' cried Bess, rubbing her hands. 'Then it is agreed. You can have Otto's wagon. Tomorrow we will move on—and your training will begin!'

✳

The companions spent that night huddled beneath the tree that shaded Otto's wagon, with Kree keeping watch above them.

The ground was cold and hard, but they preferred it to sleeping inside. Someone had taken away the mattress, the fur rug and the trunk of clothes. But, even empty, the wagon seemed haunted by memories of the pig-man and his horrible death.

Gradually, the lights around the camp were put out as people went to their rest. But just when all seemed quiet the great central fire began to burn more brightly, and low voices began chanting and singing.

The sounds went on and on. The fire blazed higher.

Several times Lief sat up. Several times he peered at the figures chanting around the roaring fire, and wondered what they were doing.

In the darkest hours of the night, the voices rose a little. For the first time, Lief heard some words clearly.

Farwall, Otto. Farwall, ald frand. Yar mask as ashas. Yar bady as dast. Naw ya dwall an ta grayt layt. Wan day way wall jayan ya. Wayt far as. Wayt far as . . .

Then, at last, he understood.

Farewell, Otto. Farewell, old friend . . . Now you dwell in the great light. One day we will join you. Wait for us. Wait for us . . .

Otto's body, and all his possessions, were being burned. The inner circle of the Masked Ones was farewelling one of its own.

Lief lay down again and pulled his blanket close around his chin. He closed his eyes. He willed himself to sleep. But when at last sleep came, leaping flames and a shapeless black figure with long white fingers haunted his dreams.

5 - Happy Vale

Just before dawn, Lief was woken by a clamour of shouting, banging and clattering. Horses were snorting. Harness was jingling.

'What is it?' he asked sleepily.

'They are preparing to leave,' said Barda, throwing aside his blanket and sitting up with a groan.

'Indeed we are,' said a sharp voice. 'And if you intend to come with us, you had better rouse yourselves.'

Rust emerged from the shadows. 'Bess sent you these,' she snapped, throwing a cloth bag on the ground. 'Put them on, and keep them on. The sight of your naked faces offends us as much as your smell.'

She turned on her heel, and left them.

'I do not think she is very fond of us,' Barda grinned. He up-ended the bag. Three masks tumbled out.

The first was a massive animal head, striped in black and yellow. The second was smaller and older, but far more exquisitely made. It was a blue-feathered bird head with a yellow beak. The third, the smallest of all, was a shapeless mass of grey fur, with a black nose and bent whiskers.

Barda put on the striped mask and was instantly transformed into a glaring stranger.

He threw the bird mask to Lief. 'This is yours, I suspect, young Lewin, since you are to be Bess's songbird,' he said.

Reluctantly, Lief pulled the blue-feathered mask over his head. To his surprise, he could hear, see and breathe far better than he had expected.

All the same, he felt uneasy. He touched his feathered face and a chill ran down his spine.

Jasmine put on the grey mask. Kree screeched and flew to a higher branch. Filli chittered anxiously.

'They do not like it,' Jasmine said sadly. 'They do not know me.'

Barda burst out laughing. 'I am not surprised!' he said. 'No-one would know you. No-one would know any of us! Why, we could travel the length and breadth of Deltora and never be recognised! This is a fine plan!'

He jumped to his feet and strode off to hitch Otto's horse to the wagon.

'I am not so sure,' Jasmine muttered. 'But—'

She broke off as an eerie, high-pitched screech floated from the direction of the field.

'What was that?' Lief gasped.

'I do not know,' Jasmine said, puzzled. Then she

shrugged, dismissing the problem from her mind.

'But in any case, we made Bess no promises,' she continued. 'We will stay with the Masked Ones only as long as it suits us.'

Lief nodded unhappily. He could not rid himself of the feeling that somehow he had lost control of his own destiny.

✳

Dawn was breaking as the wagons moved out of the forest and turned onto a rough road that ran beside the mountains.

Only the drivers rode. Everyone else walked beside the wagons, or trailed in a straggling line behind them.

Barda drove Otto's wagon. Lief and Jasmine trudged beside it. Kree flew high above, keeping them in view but never venturing close enough to be noticed.

The road became smoother and broader, and the wagons picked up speed. In another hour they passed a new sign. The Masked Ones pointed and jeered.

Lief sighed. Plainly Mad Keeth Nose, whoever he was, believed that the king chose to build bridges and roads instead of ordering more food to be grown.

If only I *could* order the crops to grow strong, and

the trees to bear fruit, he thought. If only it were that simple!

Now and again the wagons passed a tiny village. People always came running to stare and wave.

The Masked Ones would wave back. Some would juggle a few coloured balls or play a tune on a pipe. But the wagons kept moving.

'Why do we not stop?' Jasmine said, as they passed the fourth such ragged group.

'It is not worth their while to perform at small places,' sighed a woman behind them.

They turned to look at her. She was wearing a neatly made ginger cat mask. The eyes behind the mask were dull. Plainly she was one of the 'bareface hangers-on' the fox-woman had spoken of with such contempt.

'How long have you been with the Masked Ones?' Lief asked, eager to keep the conversation going.

'My man and I joined them last winter,' the woman said in a low voice. 'He does heavy work around the camp. I mend costumes and masks. Make them, too, sometimes, for once I was a fine seamstress.'

Again she sighed. 'At least we eat every day now, which is more than we did at home. But I am sick of travelling.'

'What of the mask?' Lief asked.

'Oh, I am used to that by now,' the woman said carelessly. 'Most of the time I forget I am wearing it.'

She raised her hand to her mask.

'Even at first, I did not mind it,' she said slowly. 'I

have no love for what is beneath it. And neither does my man, I am sure, whatever he says. I was branded on my cheek, in the time of the Shadow Lord. Whatever beauty I had is long gone.'

Lief said nothing. For once he was glad of his own mask. It hid the pity he knew his face must show—and what could helpless pity do but make this sad woman even sadder?

※

By mid afternoon, Lief knew they must be well into opal territory. But clearly they had crossed another border also.

They had left the budding hope of the east behind them. Gradually they had moved into the desolate realm of the Sister of the North.

Thorns tangled on the roadsides. Crops were yellow and stunted. Kree was the only bird in the sky.

Lief felt Jasmine nudging him, and looked up.

The fox-woman stood by the side of the road just ahead. When they reached her, she fell into step beside them.

'When we arrive in Happy Vale, go straight to Bess's wagon,' she said to Lief, her voice totally without expression. 'Bess wishes your training to begin at once.'

She stepped to the side of the road again and began walking rapidly towards the front of the procession without a backward glance.

※

Happy Vale turned out to be nothing like its name. The

windows of its houses, taverns and shops were filmed with dust. Dead leaves blew in the deserted streets.

The wagons of the Masked Ones creaked down the main road. Eerily, the town clock chimed four.

'Where are all the people?' Jasmine whispered.

'Dead or gone, no doubt,' the woman in the cat mask muttered. 'Bess thought that because things had begun to grow again in the east, it would be the same everywhere. She was wrong, it seems. Now, I suppose, we will have to go back the way we have come.'

Her voice was flat and listless, as if she did not care what she did.

If the Masked Ones do decide to turn back, we will have to leave them, Lief thought. Well I, for one, will be glad of it.

The line had slowed to a crawl. Lief and Jasmine craned their necks to see what was happening.

'There is a noticeboard in the town square,' Barda called down to them. 'People are slowing to read it.'

In a few more minutes they had reached the square. The first thing they passed was a fountain, which had been sealed with planks of wood. The tall clock tower rose behind it.

The noticeboard came next. As Lief looked at the notes pinned to it, his heart sank.

All the small ones seemed to speak of a life that was now ended, and a future that was never to be. The much larger notice on the right-hand side dominated them all.

Dean the Smoke will trade 3 hens for a sack of grain.

FOR SALE
These are bargains!
Fine bed. Table with 2 chairs. Kate mend-shoe

Dame Henstoke can teach you to dance. Cheap ra...

TO ALL WHO PASS THIS WAY

We, the remaining citizens of Happy Vale, have voted to leave our town and walk south-east to Parley. We have heard that there is wild food to be had in Parley, and that the spring there has begun to run clean. We heard this from Jord the knife-sharpener, who saw the wonder with his own eyes.

If you have come seeking a relative or friend from Happy Vale, you will find that person either in Parley or in the graveyard.

IMPORTANT! READ THIS!

DO NOT DRINK FROM THE FOUNTAIN! THE WATER MAKES BLISTERS ON THE TONGUE & IS FULL OF WHITE WORMS. ONLY RAINWATER IS SAFE.

Hank Modestee, who can follow orders, needs work. Ask at tavern.

IF YOU WANT TO SEND GOODS AHEAD TO PARLEY SEE ANDERS THE MEEK

Seek the Nomad! Laughing Jack your friendly travelling moneylender, is now camped at the Riverdale sign post

Lief bent his head in an agony of frustration. How many people would die, how many more towns would be abandoned, while he, Barda and Jasmine hid behind masks and dawdled towards their goal?

Travel hidden.

He ground his teeth, but knew that he had to heed Doom's warning. Secrecy was their most powerful weapon. He had to be patient.

※

Not long afterwards, they reached a field where wagons were being pulled up into a rough circle.

Masked children of all ages were already scurrying about, collecting sticks for the central fire under the stern eye of the frog-woman.

Rust the fox-woman was standing by the fence, shouting orders at some people who were unloading large red boxes from a covered cart.

Bess's wagon was on the far side of the field, beneath the overhanging branches of a tree.

'You had better be off, Lewin,' Barda said, climbing down from the wagon seat. 'We will see to things here.'

Reluctantly, Lief started across the field. As he passed the growing wood pile, a small figure carrying a towering bundle of sticks darted heedlessly across his path.

There was no way of avoiding a collision. Lief staggered and the child fell. Sticks flew everywhere.

'Watch where you are going, bird-head!' the child shouted angrily.

His small black eyes were sparkling with fury through a grinning, hairy mask. He was the boy Lief had noticed the night they were captured. The boy wearing the mask of a . . .

. . . a polypan, Lief realised, remembering the strange, thieving beast he and his companions had met on the River Tor.

The polypan-boy scrambled to his feet and began gathering his fallen sticks.

'Now I will be the last of all Plug's orphans to bring fuel for the fire,' he grumbled. 'That means I will be last in the line for food. And it is all your fault!'

'Zerry!' the frog-woman roared. 'What are you playing at, you lazy young hound?'

The boy's head jerked around. Without waiting to pick up the rest of the sticks, he shot away towards the wood pile.

'It was not me, Plug!' Lief heard him shouting as he ran. 'It was *his* fault! He tripped me!'

Lief hurried on, wondering how many of the children in the camp were orphans, taken in by the Masked Ones to be trained in their ways. Quite a number, if Zerry's words made sense.

He reached Bess's wagon and moved under the tree to the back.

The door was closed. A lumpy sack was propped against the wall beside it. The sack smelled very strongly of rotten fruit. Here and there a thin white stem poked through the rough cloth.

Curiously, Lief pinched off the tip of one of the stems and squinted at it. It was not a stem, he thought, but a root. Some sort of crop. And, by its smell, it was from the field beside the forest.

He remembered how rough the ground had felt when he was lying in the field. That was because the Masked Ones had been digging there, he thought. Digging there for five whole days!

He saw that a large, empty iron pot hung over a pile of wood nearby. Bess was planning to make soup from the white roots, it seemed. Lief wrinkled his nose at the thought of it.

He moved to the door and raised his hand to knock. Then, with a shock, he heard voices coming from inside the wagon. He pressed his ear against the door, and listened intently.

'*Yar hart as raling yar had, Bess!*' hissed a voice he recognised as that of Quill, the eagle-man.

'*Ta bay was lad ta as!*' Bess growled back. '*Ta sayns are all taya!*'

The boy was led to us, Lief translated to himself. *The signs are all there!*

'*Sayns!*' snarled Quill. '*Trackary, ya mayn! Can ya nat say at, Bess? Ta kang chays tas bay ta spay an as bacas ha laks layk Bede!*'

. . . Trickery, you mean! Can you not see it, Bess? The king chose this boy to spy on us because he looks like Bede . . .

Yes, that is just what a tyrant king would do, Lief thought uneasily. He would know that Bess was more likely to accept someone who looked like her lost son.

But why did the Masked Ones fear spies at all? What were they hiding?

'*Ya ar wrang, Quill,*' he heard Bess say coldly. '*Na, plays layv ma. Ha wal ba haya an a mamant.*'

'*Haya?*' the eagle-man thundered. '*Bat, Bess, ha wall say . . .*'

Lief's heart thumped. 'See what?' he whispered. 'What will I see?'

'*Ha wal nat naw wat ha as saying,*' snapped Bess.

He will not know what he is seeing . . .

The door of the wagon began to open. Swiftly Lief jumped back, then took two rapid steps forward, as if he was just arriving. Quill stepped out of the wagon and they almost bumped into one another.

'Oh—I beg your pardon!' Lief stammered.

The eagle man stared, then brushed passed him without a word and strode away. It was impossible to tell whether he had been deceived.

'Ah, Lewin!' Bess called from the dimness of the wagon. Suddenly her voice was warm and welcoming. 'Come in!'

6 - Mysteries

The wagon was richly furnished. The air was heavy with the scents of spices and perfumed candle wax.

Bess was sitting at the round table. A candle threw flickering light up onto her smooth owl face. Her hands were cupped around a glass ball in front of her.

'Sit down, Lewin,' she said, nodding at the chair on the other side of the table.

Unwillingly, Lief did as she asked.

'Ah,' Bess breathed. She stared, as if drinking in the sight of him.

But there is nothing to see, Lief thought. She cannot see my face. I am wearing a mask.

Then it struck him. The bird mask he was wearing must have once belonged to Bede. When Bess looked at him, she saw her son reborn.

He felt sick.

He looked down at the table. The glass ball was swirling with shadows. Was this what Quill had not wanted him to see? He thought of the Shadow Lord's crystal, and shuddered.

Bess took her hands from the ball, and the shadows disappeared.

'Do not fear the glass, Lewin,' she murmured. 'With its aid I read the signs, as my mother did before me.'

She pushed the ball away, revealing another object lying on the table in front of her. It was row of eight small metal rods fastened to a wooden base. She struck the first of the metal rods with her long fingernail and a low, clear note rang out.

'Can you name that note, Lewin?' she asked.

Lief had no idea what she meant. He shook his head.

Bess sighed. 'I feared as much,' she said. 'You have a great deal to learn.'

She passed a sheet of paper to him. 'Music is like another language,' she said. 'This is how we write it down.'

'Now, I am going to play the notes on this paper,' Bess said. 'Listen carefully.'

She struck the rods one by one. Notes rang out, going up like stairs from low to high. She played them again, this time singing their names.

Lief's fingers felt hot. He looked down and saw that the liquid that had oozed from the fragment of root was drying to grey jelly. His fingertips were stinging. Suddenly fearful, he rubbed them against his coat. The grey jelly peeled from his skin in tiny balls, which he brushed quickly onto the floor.

'Stop fidgeting and pay attention, Lewin!' snapped Bess. 'You *must* learn to read and write music. How else will you be able to note down the beautiful songs you will compose for me, as Bede used to do?'

Lief's face grew hot beneath his mask.

'Bess—' he mumbled. But Bess's voice flowed on as if he had not spoken.

'Ah, Bede's songs could charm the birds from the trees,' she sighed. 'The words were full of feeling. The rhymes were perfect. The melodies were charming. And, of course, his voice was without compare. Wherever we went, silly village girls were drawn to him like bees to a honeypot.'

She laughed. 'They paid well for the chance to swoon over Bede! When we moved on, we would leave a trail of broken hearts behind us, and our purses would be heavy with bareface gold.'

She reached across the table and took Lief's hand. 'And you will be the same, Lewin,' she said. 'You will restore the fortunes of the Masked Ones!'

Lief winced, glad that the mask was hiding his face.

'Bess, I will never be like Bede,' he said awkwardly. 'And—I do not want to be.'

He tried to free his hand, but Bess held it fast.

'Trust me, Lewin,' she said. 'This was fated to be.'

Lief shook his head.

'Yes!' Bess insisted. 'I lost Bede seven years ago. I had grown used to my grief. But lately, thoughts of him have haunted me. The glass kept showing me his face. I did not know why. I feared I was losing my reason!'

She freed Lief's hand and drew the glass ball towards her again. She bent over it, gazing hungrily.

'But then—then you came, Lewin,' she murmured. 'You came into our secret place, through our barriers, guarded by a phantom. A boy so like Bede. A boy who could speak our language! I saw the signs, and realised what they meant. My thoughts of Bede had been preparation for the coming of his replacement. You!'

She tapped the huge gold ring on her little finger. It was the only ring that had no stone. Its broad surface was covered in carved signs.

'This ring is worn by the leader of the Masked Ones,' she said softly. 'One day, it will be yours. You must work hard to be worthy, for in the hand of the leader lies the gift of life . . . and death.'

Lief did not trust himself to speak.

Bess was wrong, so wrong. Her 'signs' were only matters of chance. As she would realise, if only he could tell her the truth.

But he could not tell her. Not if he valued his life, and the lives of his companions.

Bess was waiting for him to speak. He blurted out the first thing that came into his head.

'Bess, what happened to Bede?'

For a moment, he thought she was not going to answer. Then she spoke.

'Seven years ago, when we were last in the north-west, Grey Guards attacked our wagons,' she said. 'Eight of the inner circle died defending us.'

Her enormous hands were clasped on the tabletop, the rings biting deep into the flesh of her straining fingers.

'The Guards were killed, but we knew that soon more would come. We fled to a village deep in the mountains. It is a lonely place, but we had visited it only the year before, and knew the way. So we went—to Bede's doom.'

'What is its name, this village?' Lief asked softly. His scalp was tingling.

'You would not know it,' said Bess. 'It is not worth knowing. They call it Shadowgate.'

Lief sat frozen. Can *this*, too, be chance? he thought. Or can it be that Bess is right after all? Can it be that all this is somehow meant?

The memory of the dragon's voice whispered in his mind. *This is the place where I must leave you . . . I feel it.*

'There are beasts, deep in the mountains,' Bess muttered. 'Monsters beyond imagining. Things that crawl in the shadows. Things that growl deep below the rock. Shadowgate lies among them. A dread pass is the only way to reach it. We hid our tracks, disguised our scent, so the Guards could not smell us out.'

She drew a deep, shuddering breath. 'We hid in Shadowgate for a full month. I wanted to make sure we were safe. And safe we were—though the villagers did not welcome us. But there was another danger I had not expected.'

Lief wet his lips. 'What happened?' he asked.

'Bede . . . lost his heart,' said Bess. 'To a silly bareface girl not worthy to tie the strings on his shoes.'

The bitterness in her voice was chilling.

'I suspected nothing,' she went on. 'He and the scheming wench had been meeting in secret. He came to me the night before his eighteenth birthday. The mask of his adulthood was ready. The ceremony of his entry to the inner circle was planned for the morning. He said he wished to leave the Masked Ones—to become a travelling minstrel, and marry this—Mariette.'

She spoke the name like a curse.

'I could not believe my ears,' she hissed. 'I said, "You will quickly tire of this ignorant little bareface! Why, only last year you were dallying with her sister—that proud beauty, Kirsten, who ran off into the mountains in shame when you left her, and caused these villagers to hate us."'

She snorted, as though Kirsten's fate was no concern of hers.

'But Bede told me that he had always preferred Mariette to her sister. He said it had begun as a fancy, but that in this past month he had learned what true love was. He said he could not live without the girl. He talked wildly, like one in a fever.'

So, Lief thought grimly. Bede was caught in the net he had so often set for others. There is justice in that.

But Bess, lost in memories, did not seem to be aware of what he could see so clearly.

'I told him to put the girl out of his mind,' she said. 'I told him, "You are a Masked One. We do not marry outsiders. Tomorrow, you will put on the mask of your adulthood, and that will be the end of it."'

She sighed.

'He seemed to accept it. He left me gently, with a kiss. But I never saw him again. That night, he and the girl ran away into the mountains. We searched, but we could not find them.'

The brown owl face showed no expression. Only the trembling voice gave a sign that Bess was re-living an old, terrible grief.

'The mountains had swallowed them up, just as they had swallowed the girl's sister the year before,' she said. 'And so Bede threw his life away, and we lost our greatest treasure.'

And what of the parents who lost two daughters because of your son, Bess? Lief thought, as her voice trailed away. Have you no word for them?

The silence lengthened. Then, at last, Bess seemed

to rouse herself. She straightened her shoulders.

'I have work to do,' she said abruptly, pushing the little row of metal rods towards Lief. 'I expect you to know all your notes by tomorrow morning.'

Lief stood up, pushed the chimes and the paper into his pocket, and left the wagon. He was determined that by morning he, Barda and Jasmine would be long gone.

Outside, the sun was setting and shadows were gathering behind the line of wagons. Lief breathed in the fresh, cool air with relief.

It was quiet where he was standing, but the centre of the field was full of movement. All around the unlit wood heap, Masked Ones were practising their skills.

The frog-woman was juggling flaming torches. Three clowns were tumbling about blowing coloured bubbles from enormous pipes. The eagle-man, Quill, was standing with Barda, who was lifting a set of enormous weights. A man with the head of a lizard was doing magic tricks, assisted by the polypan-boy, Zerry.

To one side, a group of blue-clad acrobats with dog faces were standing on one another's shoulders to form a tall pyramid. Balanced at the top of the pyramid was a small, grey-masked figure, standing on its hands.

It was Jasmine. She had put aside her clumsy coat, and her feet were bare.

Lief caught his breath as she turned a backwards somersault and landed upright on the shoulders of the man at the pyramid's tip.

'Your brother is a talented acrobat, it seems,' a low

voice said in Lief's ear.

Lief jumped, turned, and saw the fox-woman standing very close to him. He had not heard her approach. Perhaps she had been standing there in the shadows all along.

'Oh—yes,' Lief stammered.

'It is hard to believe he has never been trained,' the fox-woman went on smoothly. Her eyes were narrow with suspicion.

'Jay is self-taught,' Lief answered, with perfect truth. His eyes flicked around the field. And it was then that he noticed the fluttering white patches that dotted the fences on all sides.

He turned and looked behind him. Yes, the fence there was covered with white splashes too. Poison-spitting moths clung to the rough wood, silently opening and closing their wings.

Lief remembered the red boxes he had seen being unloaded by the fence. The moths had been in those boxes, no doubt. Now they were in place. There would be no escape from the camp tonight.

He clenched his fists. The disappointment was bitter. He heard a distant screech, as if Kree was echoing his feelings.

'Is something wrong?' Rust asked coldly.

'No,' Lief managed to say. 'No, I—'

His voice was drowned out by a high, wavering shriek of pure terror.

7 - Phantom

Everything seemed to stop. The figures around the wood pile froze where they stood. The music faltered and died.

The terrified scream came again, dissolving into a ghastly, rasping gurgle.

His heart pounding, Lief began to run between the wagons and the fence, following the sound.

With Rust close behind him he pounded past wagon after wagon, dodging stamping, terrified horses, leaping over boxes and piles of belongings.

Otto's wagon was ahead. The door was hanging open, swinging crazily on its hinges as if blown by a gale.

And rising against the shadow of the door, rising up, up, so that at last it was outlined against the orange sky, was a deeper shadow—something black and billowing, with long white fingers that glimmered in the dark. Where its face should have been there was a flat gleam of green.

On the ground by the wagon's back wheels, sprawled over a half-empty pack and a tangle of clothes, lay a twisted shape.

Lief's throat closed. Behind him, the fox-woman cried out. And in that moment, the black thing writhed, thinned, and was gone.

The wagon door slammed shut with a crash. Lief ran forward and bent over the sprawled figure.

It was the woman in the cat mask—the woman he and Jasmine had spoken to on the road to Happy Vale.

One side of her mask was scorched. Smoke drifted from the blackened patch, and there was the ghastly smell of burned hair and flesh. The staring eyes seemed filled with horror, and the teeth were bared in a snarl of fear.

'It is the seamstress, Fern!' whispered Rust. She sounded horrified, but the horror was also plainly mixed with relief.

She is grateful that it was not a member of the inner circle, but only a 'bareface hanger-on' who was attacked, Lief thought grimly. Gently he slipped his fingers beneath the neck of the cat mask, feeling for a pulse.

His stomach turned over as the staring eyes focused on him, and the lips moved. The burned woman was still alive! She was trying to speak. Lief leaned closer.

Words came to him, faint as breath. 'I . . . am . . . sorry. I . . . was . . . so . . . afraid.'

'What is she saying?' cried Rust. 'Is she—?'

Angrily Lief waved his free hand to quiet her. 'Be at peace now,' he whispered to the dying woman.

The pulse beneath his fingers was light and fluttering. The agonised eyes held his, filled with urgent appeal. The lips moved again. 'Beware . . . the Masked One . . .' the woman breathed. 'Beware . . .'

The voice died away. The eyes grew fixed. The fluttering pulse stopped.

Lief waited for a moment, then drew back.

'She is gone,' he said quietly. He began to pull the cat mask from the dead woman's face.

'Don't!' Rust gasped behind him.

Lief took no notice. He uncovered a scorched neck, and then a pale face. One cheek was deeply burned. The brand of the Shadow Lord shone blood red in the centre of the blackened skin. Lief could feel the heat still rising from it.

It is as if the burning came from within, he thought. His skin crawled.

'Cover her face, for pity's sake!' hissed Rust. 'The others are coming.'

Lief became aware of shouting and the pounding of approaching feet. He looked around, saw a blanket lying nearby amid a jumble of clothes, and threw it over the body.

The crowd was nearly upon them. Rust ran to the front of Otto's wagon, and held up her arms.

'Go back to work!' she shouted. 'There is nothing

to see. There has been an accident, that is all.'

She folded her arms and stood immoveable till at last the crowd did her bidding and began moving back to the centre of the field.

Barda and Jasmine stayed. Rust seemed to know that there was no point in trying to make them go.

✳

Bess's reaction to Fern's death shocked them all.

'The woman was stealing from your wagon, Lewin,' she said, shrugging. 'She paid the price.'

'What do you mean?' Lief exclaimed, horrified.

'Something watches over you, Lewin,' said Bess dreamily, moving her hands over the glass ball. 'Anyone who tries to injure you is in danger.'

The fox-woman stirred uneasily. 'Bess, I do not think—' she began.

'Rust, see that Fern is buried without delay,' Bess said, without looking at her. 'And decently, with her mask in place, as is proper. Keep to your story of an accident. The people may turn against Lewin if they know the truth.'

Lief opened his mouth to protest, but Barda gripped his arm warningly, and he remained silent.

Barda is right, he thought. Better to say nothing. If Bess really believes that I am protected by some sort of spirit, it may help us later. If she does not—if the thing that killed Fern is some hideous secret she and the rest of the inner circle share—defying her will only put us in even greater danger.

When Fern's body had been moved, Rust left the companions alone to re-pack their scattered belongings. At last they could speak freely.

Jasmine called Kree to her and began tending to the wound on the back of his neck. He squawked and clucked as she cleaned the raw place and smeared it with more of the green ointment.

'Kree says he saw it all,' Jasmine said in a low voice. 'Fern came and began searching our packs. He was trying to decide what to do when the phantom appeared from the shadows and attacked her.'

'"Beware the Masked One",' Barda frowned. 'Are you sure Fern did not say "the Masked *Ones*", Lief?'

'I am sure,' Lief said slowly. 'She meant only one person. If only she had given a name! Then we could have told Bess which of her people is conjuring up the phantom. Whoever it is, is growing stronger. The thing was clearer this time. It had more shape. And its face— or whatever horror was inside its hood—gleamed green.'

'The sorcerer may be Bess herself,' said Barda. 'She said the phantom watches over you. And both its victims were intent on doing you harm.'

'But when Otto was attacked, Bess did not even know I existed!' Lief objected.

'Still, both deaths were certainly connected with us,' Jasmine said. The sorcerer must be someone who wants to drive us away from the troupe.'

'We have a wide choice, then,' growled Barda. 'The whole of the inner circle, except Bess, wants us gone.'

'Well, as far as I am concerned, they can have their wish,' Lief said flatly. 'Let us tell Bess that we wish to leave at once—and tell her in front of others. That is the best way of ensuring our safety, and the safety of everyone else here.'

'It is,' Jasmine agreed. 'And I, for one, will be very glad to go.'

'I, too,' said Barda. 'Though I do not relish the idea of telling Bess.'

✳

By the time the village clock struck ten, it was as if the attack had never happened.

Fern the seamstress had been buried. Fern's grieving husband had been given a potion and had fallen into a drugged sleep. Life in the camp had returned to normal. And Lief, Barda and Jasmine were again sitting at the purple-draped table outside Bess's wagon, while Kree kept silent watch in the tree above their heads.

They were eating dinner, served once again by Rust. The meal was nearly finished, but still they had not spoken of what was most on their minds. Then, suddenly, Bess gave them their chance.

'This has been a hard day,' she said, spooning the last of her soup into her mouth. 'The new people—especially the orphans—are growing restless. We need a performance to lift their spirits—to make them know how fine it is to be a Masked One.'

She sighed heavily. 'Plainly we must forget our plans to perform here. We must go east to Purley, I fear.

I have never liked the place, but at least we know that we will have a good audience there.'

Barda cleared his throat. 'What a great pity!' he said. 'If you are returning to the east, I fear that we must part company with you.'

'What?' Bess dropped her spoon with a clatter. 'But you cannot leave us! Lewin has a great future before him. You, too, Berry, from all I have heard. And even young Jay—'

'Ah, well, it cannot be helped,' Barda said firmly. 'As you know, my nephews and I have always planned to go to the west.'

Lief glanced at Rust. Her eyes were shining with amazed relief.

You did not expect this, did you, Rust? he thought. You were so sure we were spies, and would cling to the troupe as long as we could. Well, you were wrong. Soon you will be rid of us. And we will be rid of you!

Bess was panting, as if she had been running. She turned to Lief.

'Surely you do not want this, do you, Lewin?' she demanded.

'I am sorry, Bess, but my first loyalty must be to my uncle,' Lief said, grateful that he did not have to hurt her even further by admitting he wanted to leave. 'Wherever he goes, I must go too.'

Bess bowed her head, struggling to calm herself. 'Well,' she mumbled. 'This has been a great shock.'

At last she looked up. 'But perhaps it is all for the

best,' she said, smiling bravely. 'Bring a jug of wildberry wine, if you please, Rust. Berry needs restoring. Quill worked him far too hard this afternoon. And bring some oatcakes with honey for the young ones.'

The fox-woman nodded and hurried away, taking the used dishes from the table with her. Clearly she was in high good humour.

'Lewin,' Bess said, 'I have a favour to ask of you.'

'What is it, Bess?' asked Lief cautiously.

'I want you to go into my wagon, and take the round silver box from beneath my bed,' Bess said. 'In the box, you will find a mask. I want you to put that mask on, Lewin, and wear it for me.'

Lief's stomach turned over.

'I see by your eyes that you have guessed,' Bess said. 'Yes. It is the mask of Bede's adulthood—the mask he never wore. It would have been yours one day, Lewin, if you had stayed with us.'

She looked down at her folded hands. 'Now that will never be,' she said. 'But it would give me such joy to see you wear it—just for a single hour—on this, our last night together.'

Lief hesitated. He could feel Barda and Jasmine staring at him. No doubt they could see no harm in Bess's request.

And what *was* the harm?

He stood up. 'If it would please you, Bess,' he said.

He took a lantern from the collection around the table, and moved to the back of the wagon.

The sack that had stood by the door now sagged half empty. A fire burned beneath the black iron pot, which was filled with slowly bubbling liquid that looked like porridge, but smelled strongly of rotten fruit.

Lief wrinkled his nose. Plainly, Bess was cooking some of the roots from the secret field.

I am glad we are leaving tomorrow, if that is to be the Masked Ones' dinner tomorrow night, he thought.

He entered the wagon, went quickly to the bed and soon found the silver box.

Inside, wrapped in yellow silk, was a magnificent mask—a gleaming blue bird-head, similar to the one he was wearing, but much finer and more lifelike.

Lief reached out and touched it. It seemed to quiver beneath his fingers. For a single, horrible moment it seemed alive. Lief snatched his hand away, his heart beating wildly. He clutched at the Belt of Deltora, hidden beneath his clothes.

Gradually his panic ebbed away. He forced himself to look down.

The mask lay in its bed of silk—a beautiful, lifeless thing of feathers, fabric and paste.

Filled with shame, Lief took off his old mask. At the same moment, the village clock began striking eleven. The sound seemed so loud and clear!

For a few moments he relished his freedom. Then, as the last, ringing chime died away, he gritted his teeth, picked up the new mask, and pulled it on.

8 - Tricks

The mask felt soft and cool against Lief's skin. It was so light that he could barely feel it. It moulded itself to his face and neck as though it had been made for him. It was almost like wearing no mask at all.

Suddenly he felt more cheerful. He let himself out of the wagon and strode back to where Bess, Barda and Jasmine were waiting.

Bess was lying back in her chair with her eyes closed, but Barda and Jasmine turned to look at him.

Jasmine started, her eyes wide. Barda gave a muffled gasp, and half-rose from his stool.

'What is wrong?' Lief asked, confused.

Jasmine swallowed. 'You look—you look as if you are half bird,' she whispered. 'That mask . . .'

'I have never seen anything like it,' said Barda, sinking back onto the stool again. 'It made the hair rise on the back of my neck!'

Feeling quite pleased at the excitement he had caused, Lief sat down.

Bess's eyes fluttered open. They focused on him, widened, and seemed to glow.

'Ah,' she breathed. 'Thank you, Lewin. You have made an old woman very happy. Wear it for an hour— till midnight. That will be enough.'

She rubbed her hands. 'Now!' she said. 'Let me entertain you!'

The companions looked at her blankly, and she laughed.

'Do you think that the Masked Ones have only acrobats, singers and clowns to offer?' she cried, waving at the people practising by the central fire. 'Why, we can do far more than that! I, for example, can read minds!'

'Is that so?' asked Barda dryly.

'Indeed,' said Bess. 'But to do it I must have my trusty glass!'

Grunting with effort, she bent and lifted from the ground the glass ball Lief had last seen in her wagon. She placed the ball in the centre of the table.

'Now, who is to be my subject?' she asked. 'Berry? Are you willing?'

'Certainly,' agreed Barda, grinning broadly. 'But I warn you—no one who has ever tried it has been able to read my mind. My skull is too thick, perhaps.'

'Then I will begin with something simple,' Bess said calmly. 'Think of a number between one and nine. Make your nephews aware of what it is, if you wish, but do not tell me.'

Barda shrugged. 'Very well,' he said. 'I have it.'

Below the table top, where Bess could not see, he held up five fingers, telling Lief and Jasmine that the number he had chosen was five.

'Concentrate on the number, all of you,' said Bess. 'Try to think of nothing else.'

She held her hands just above the glass ball. She closed her eyes and began to chant in a low, sing-song voice.

The table top seemed to rise slightly. Then, slowly, it began to spin. The purple cloth shimmered as it moved, its hem whispering as it brushed the dusty grass. The glass ball turned in the centre, winking in the candlelight.

Lief felt a chill run down his spine. He knew this must be a trick, but the sight was eerie. Bess is a good actor, he thought.

Bess's blind owl face loomed over the turning table. Her hands, with their many flashing rings, cast shadows on the winking glass ball.

No doubt she has done this a thousand times, Lief thought. As her mother did before her. And her grandmother and great-grandmother too, no doubt.

Suddenly he was filled with a strange sort of pride to be among these talented people, sharing their life. Almost, he regretted that he had to leave them so soon.

'The visions are hazy,' Bess murmured. 'I cannot

see clearly. Someone's mind is wandering.'

She shook her head impatiently. 'That number is no good to me now. I will have to try again. Berry— double the number! Then—then multiply it by—by five! The answer is your new number.'

'Very well,' Barda said. He glanced at Lief and Jasmine, who nodded. The new number was fifty.

They were all concentrating hard now, but Bess shook her head again.

'I cannot understand it!' she muttered to herself. 'Why can I not see it?'

She seemed really distressed. Lief began to feel sorry for her.

'Divide your new number by the number you first thought of,' Bess ordered, frantically moving her hands over the glass ball.

Ten, Lief thought. Fifty divided by five is ten.

Bess drew a deep breath. Her hands slowed.

'Better,' she said softly. 'Now, take away—ah yes!— take away seven, the number of magic! And then concentrate—concentrate hard on the number that remains.'

Ten minus seven, thought Lief. Three. Three . . . three . . . three . . .

The table slowed, and became still.

'Ah . . . at last!' Bess breathed. 'I see it! The number in your minds is . . .three!'

Lief, Barda and Jasmine exclaimed and clapped.

'Amazing!' cried Barda. 'How did you do it?'

Bess shrugged and straightened her shawls. 'Who am I to try to explain the mysterious power of the glass?' she said solemnly. But her eyes were twinkling behind her mask.

And suddenly, thinking over what had happened, Lief realised that she had been acting all the time. Her pretended hesitation and distress had disguised a very simple trick.

If you multiply a number by two and then by five, you are really multiplying it by ten! he thought. So if you then divide your total by the original number, ten will always be your answer. Take away seven from ten— and you are left with three.

So that was how Bess had 'read' their minds. Whichever number they started with, the end result would be three, every time!

He smiled beneath his mask.

'The spinning table top is not so mysterious,' Jasmine said boldly. 'I have seen something a little like it before. I am sure you make it move by working a pedal under the table.'

Bess laughed heartily. 'You are not easily impressed, young Jay,' she said. 'But of course you are right. I can make the table move and stop again with the slightest tap of my foot. It is just a little trick—to make the performance more interesting.'

'It does that,' said Barda. 'But I still do not understand how—'

'Ah, here are our drinks at last!' Bess cried. She took

the glass ball and set it carefully on the ground beside her chair.

Rust appeared carrying a loaded tray. 'I fear there is no honey, Bess,' she said, bending to place two small cakes, two cups and a stone jug on the table. 'The last jar has disappeared from the food wagon. That young thief, Zerry, took it, no doubt. I do not know why you put up with him!'

'Zerry has very light fingers,' Bess agreed calmly, taking the cork from the jug and filling the cups with deep red wine. 'After all, he has lived by thieving ever since he could walk.'

She handed one of the cups to Barda. 'But that is just why I wanted him, Rust. If he can take a purse from a man's coat, without that man noticing, he can learn to deceive an audience with ease. He will be a great magician one day.'

Rust sniffed and straightened up, tucking the empty tray under her arm.

'Perhaps,' she said darkly. 'Though Plug says that he neglects his lessons, preferring to spend time with the horses. Perhaps—' She broke off, and her hand flew to her mouth.

She was staring at Lief, her eyes bulging with shock.

'Ah, you have noticed Lewin's mask at last,' said Bess lightly. 'Does it not suit him?'

'Bess!' The fox-woman's voice was a strangled whisper. 'Bess, you cannot—'

'You know better than to tell me what I can and

cannot do, Rust!' Bess growled. 'Leave us at once!'

The fox-woman ducked her head and stumbled away.

There was an awkward silence. Then Bess sighed.

'We must not let poor Rust spoil our pleasure,' she said. 'She respects our old traditions far too well, and will not see that rules must change with the times.'

She lifted her cup.

'Good health!' she said, and drank deeply.

'Good health!' Barda repeated. He sipped his own wine and smacked his lips. 'Very good!' he said.

From his pocket he took the little carved box that he had been trying to open ever since he came by it in the Os-Mine Hills. A small rod of polished wood protruded from one of the sides, very near the top. He passed the box to Bess.

'Here is a puzzle for you,' he said. 'I thought I had solved it, but there is more than one lock. Would you like to try your skill?'

Bess took the little box in her enormous hands and turned it over with interest. Barda watched, grinning, as she pressed the carving here and there. He had spent hours working on the box in Broome. He was sure she would not be able to open it.

Lief moved restlessly, glancing over his shoulder at the activity around the central fire. He longed to go and join the crowd.

Bess glanced up. 'You young ones run along and watch the entertainments for a time, if you wish,' she said kindly. 'Take your cakes with you. Berry and I will be cosy together here.'

Lief and Jasmine stood up with relief, picked up their cakes and left the table. From his perch in the tree, Kree silently watched them go.

'Bess is being very pleasant to Uncle Berry,' Jasmine said in a low voice, breaking off part of her cake and cautiously slipping it beneath her jacket for Filli. 'Do you think she hopes to change his mind about leaving?'

'Perhaps,' Lief said absent-mindedly. He quickened his steps. He could not wait to become part of the life around the fire.

Together he and Jasmine plunged into the crowd. Jasmine was soon claimed by the dog-faced acrobats, who were forming their pyramid again. Lief wandered on alone in a happy dream, drinking in the amazing sights and sounds around him.

Jugglers, singers, musicians, magicians . . . Here a dragon-man breathing fire. There a tall thin man with the glistening head of a snake, tying himself in knots. Beside him, a squirrel-woman dancing with bare feet on a bed of hot coals . . .

Two girls in furry masks like Jasmine's walked casually by on stilts.

'Bess says I will be given the mask of my adulthood very soon,' Lief heard one of them say to the other. 'It will be a water bird, as I requested. At last! I have been eighteen for months!'

'You are lucky, Neelie,' said the other girl enviously.

'Imagine! You will not have to live with the orphans any more. I am sick and tired of old frog-face Plug!'

'Never mind,' the first girl laughed. 'You will be eighteen in summer, Lin. Then it will be your turn. Bess is very pleased by how hard we worked in the Field of Masks. She says she has enough purebond roots now to make many new adult masks. Enough for all the orphans as they come of age.'

They strode on, weaving gracefully through the crowd.

So—that is one mystery solved, in any case, Lief thought, fascinated. The roots from the field are not food. They are boiled until they dissolve, and Bess uses the mixture to make the inner skin of the special adulthood masks. It must be an ancient craft. No wonder its secrets are closely guarded.

He smiled after the girls, who were still chattering happily. How good it is to be among my own people, he found himself thinking. How wonderful to be part of this world . . . to have this feeling of safety and belonging. How wonderful, to be a Masked One . . .

But you are not really a Masked One, a small, clear voice said in his head. You are not part of this world at all. And you do not want to be! Only a few hours ago you could not wait to get away from it. Remember?

Lief tried to push the voice aside, but it would not leave him. As though it had made a gap in his mind through which a cold breeze blew, he shivered.

Suddenly he noticed Rust, Quill and Plug standing

nearby. They were watching him, talking in low voices. When they saw him looking, they quickly turned away.

Lief felt a sudden pang of grief. Then he shook his head impatiently. Why should he care if they rejected him? Why should he long to be accepted as one of them?

Why could he not stop shivering?

The crowd surged around him. Waves of music battered him. A group of masked children playing some chasing game surrounded him, jostled him, laughed shrilly and ran on. The little apprentice magician, Zerry, was among them.

I hope Rust did not see you, Zerry, Lief thought, looking down at his honey-smeared jacket. You would do well to keep away from her—at least until you have washed your hands.

The crowd parted a little, and he caught a glimpse of Jasmine swinging on a high bar with three of the blue-clad acrobats. She seemed as far away from him as if she was on the moon. In the distance, in front of Bess's wagon, he could see the figures of Barda and Bess still sitting at the table.

Bess was passing the puzzle box back to Barda. By her actions, and Barda's laughter, Lief realised that she had managed to find and release a second lock, but the box still had not opened. He smiled, watching.

Bess fumbled, and the box fell onto the ground.

Barda bent to pick it up.

And, as quickly as a striking snake, Bess leaned across the table and tipped something into his cup.

9 - Terror

For a split second Lief stared, hardly able to believe his eyes. It had all happened so quickly! He had seen no bottle or jar in Bess's hand.

But he had clearly seen a stream of white powder fall into the cup. He had seen it!

A wave of horror flooded through him. Frantically he began to fight his way through the crowd towards Bess's wagon.

Bess is a good actor . . .

Oh, yes, Bess is a good actor, he thought wildly. Good enough to convince us that she had given in gracefully. Good enough to laugh and joke with Barda while coldly planning his death.

He groaned aloud as he remembered what he had said to Bess.

. . . my first loyalty must be to my uncle . . . Wherever he goes, I must go too.

Those words had signed Barda's death warrant.

For Bess, it had all been very simple. Berry stood between Lewin and Bess. So Berry must die.

The crowd parted briefly and Lief saw that Barda was back in his chair again. Bess was pouring more wine into his cup and her own.

'Barda!' Lief roared. 'Do not drink!'

But it was useless! His voice was drowned by the crowd's noise.

Animal and bird heads loomed all around him like things out of nightmare. Clowns capered foolishly in front of him, barring his way. He dodged around them, and cannoned into the girls on stilts.

With a shrill scream, one of the girls toppled and fell, crashing down on a group of jugglers.

That attracted Bess and Barda's attention. Lief saw Barda turn. He saw Bess peer at the crowd, one hand shading her eyes. He saw Kree flutter down from the tree like a black shadow.

Frantically Lief shouted and waved. But Bess and Barda were looking at the girl, who was scrambling unsteadily to her feet while the jugglers crawled around her, picking up the balls they had dropped. Kree was nowhere to be seen.

Again the crowd closed in. Lief put his head down and pushed forward desperately, thrusting people aside, ignoring their angry protests.

'Make way!' he shouted. 'Make way!'

'Make way yourself, you rude young pup!' snarled

a man in a ragged bear mask. He pushed Lief violently between the shoulder blades.

Lief lurched forward and crashed, sprawling, to the ground. All the breath was knocked from his body. Coughing and gasping he crawled to his knees, shaking his head to clear it.

He had been thrown out of the crowd. Ahead he could see clear ground. He could see the wagon beneath the tree, and the two people sitting at the purple-covered table, ringed with lanterns.

Barda and Bess had picked up their cups and were raising them in a toast.

'No!' Lief gasped.

They both threw their heads back, and drank.

'No!' Lief croaked in agony. 'No! *Barda!*'

He staggered to his feet and began to run.

It was as though everything was moving very slowly. As though he was seeing everything through a bright mist.

He reached the table, the breath wheezing in his chest. Barda turned to look at him. Bess half rose, her smooth owl face expressionless.

'What is wrong?' Barda exclaimed in alarm.

'Lewin!' Bess cried, at the same moment. 'I fear your uncle is not well. His efforts today strained his heart and—'

She broke off. Her golden eyes widened and filled with what seemed like surprise. She looked down at her cup still clutched in her hand.

Her fingers jerked. The cup fell onto the table, spun and lay still.

Then she fell back, clutching her chest.

Barda exclaimed and jumped up, the stool tipping and falling behind him.

Stunned, Lief stared down at the table—at Bess's fallen cup. From its lip, the last drops of wine trickled onto the purple tablecloth—gleaming red wine, mixed with a pale sludge of white powder.

'She drank the poison herself!' he whispered. 'But how—?'

Then he looked up—up at the tree that stretched above them. Kree was back on his perch on the lowest branch. He was very still. But his yellow eyes were gleaming.

I can make the table turn and stop again with the slightest tap of my foot.

So Bess had said. They had all heard her, including Kree. No doubt Kree had reasoned that the slightest tap of a strong beak like his would work just as well.

And so it had. Lief remembered the moment when the girl on stilts had fallen. Both Bess and Barda had looked towards the crowd. And that had been the moment Kree had been waiting for. While their attention was distracted, he had flown down from his perch, hopped under the table and done what he had to do.

The table top had turned. The cups had been reversed. Bess had drunk her own poison.

Masked Ones from the edges of the crowd were

running towards them, realising that something was wrong. They stood gaping as their leader lay back fighting for breath.

Barda had sprung to Bess's side, and was bending over her. 'It must be her heart!' he shouted. 'She needs air!'

He began tearing at Bess's mask.

'No!' Bess muttered, her hands moving feebly, trying to push Barda's away. 'No . . .'

With a tiny click, the top of the golden ring on her little finger fell open like a lid. A few grains of white powder still clung to the sides of the cavity revealed within.

This ring is worn by the leader of the Masked Ones . . .

Lief stared, Bess's words echoing in his mind. Words he now truly understood.

In the hand of the leader lies the gift of life . . . and death.

'Lief! I cannot get her mask off. My fingers are too clumsy. Help me!' Barda's voice was agonised.

Lief moved stiffly to his side. He knew that it was useless. He knew that Bess was doomed. But still he grasped the feathers at the base of her mask and pulled upwards with all his strength.

Bess shrieked in agony.

Startled, Lief looked down at his fingers.

They were red with blood. Blood was streaming from beneath the torn rim of the mask's base, trickling down Bess's neck, soaking into the silk of her purple dress . . .

He met Barda's horrified eyes.

'The mask will not come off,' he muttered, through chattering teeth. 'It is part of her. Joined to her. It will not . . .'

He backed away, holding his bloody hands out in front of him.

A woman in the crowd screamed hysterically.

'What are you doing?' shouted the voice of the fox-woman behind them. 'Get away from her! Bess! Oh, Bess!'

In seconds, the members of the Masked Ones' inner circle were pushing Lief and Barda aside, clustering around Bess, trying to hide her from the gathering crowd.

But it was too late. Everyone had seen.

'Blood! He tried to pull the mask off—and her skin tore away with it!' a high voice shrieked. 'The mask has grown into her face! Oh—oh, horrible! Horrible!'

There was a chorus of shuddering groans, wails of horror.

Lief looked around him. Everywhere, terrified people were tearing off their own masks and throwing them to the ground, trampling them underfoot. Faces were revealed, strangely shocking in their nakedness— faces old and young, pretty and plain, filled with disgust, with horror, with fear.

The man who had worn the bear mask was small-eyed and red-faced. Foam had gathered at the corners of his mouth.

'It is the same with all of them!' he howled, pointing at the Masked Ones gathered around Bess. 'Freaks! Sorcerers! Kill them!'

The crowd surged forward, then halted, wavering. Silence fell.

The members of the inner circle had turned. Every one of them held a long, narrow knife.

Shoulder to shoulder they faced the bareface crowd, and their eyes were filled with loathing. Proudly they lifted their heads—their heads covered by the masks which were part of them.

The masks of their adulthood, Lief thought dazedly. Put on at the age of eighteen. Bonded to their flesh, forever . . . forever . . .

In the stillness, the village clock began to chime.

One . . . two . . .

Lief looked over the heads of the Masked Ones, beyond the tree to where the clock tower stood, shining in the moonlight. The hands of the clock were pointing straight upwards.

Midnight.

The skin of his face and neck seemed to warm and prickle. The memory of Bess's voice whispered in his mind.

Wear it for one hour—till midnight. That will be enough.

He looked down again. The eagle-man, Quill, met his eyes. 'You had better join us, Lewin of Broome,' Quill said quietly. 'Like it or not, you are one of us, now.'

Yes.

Lief took a step forward. Then, suddenly, his arms were seized, and he was jerked back. Bewildered, he turned his head from one side to the other. Jasmine and Barda each held one of his arms. They were holding him, shaking him, calling to him.

Lief recoiled. Jasmine and Barda had taken off their masks. Their mouths seemed to writhe horribly as they shouted. Their naked faces were beaded with sweat, creased and twisted with horror.

They were ugly—disgusting. It made him sick to look at them.

He struggled vainly to free himself. Barda and Jasmine were still shouting, but he could not understand what they were saying. The chiming of the clock filled his mind.

Five . . . six . . .

'You see?' roared the voice of the red-faced man. 'See the boy in the bird mask? Bess the witch favoured him! She changed him into one of them! And so she would have changed us all, at last! Turned us into freaks, like herself!'

Shouting angrily, the crowd surged forward again. Some had armed themselves with rocks, and with flaming sticks from the fire.

'Burn them!' a woman shrieked.

The Masked Ones stood their ground.

'Rust!' Quill said.

Rust cupped her hands around her mouth. Her fox-face gleamed in the candlelight as she drew breath. Then she gave an unearthly, high-pitched screech.

It was like the weird cry Lief and Jasmine had heard in the forest camp of the Masked Ones. And now they knew its purpose.

For from the fences around the field the giant moths rose in a cloud.

Like thousands of scraps of paper whirling in a breeze, the moths swarmed towards the one who had called them in.

But there were no red boxes ready to receive them. They could not land. Confused, they swooped over the crowd, a fluttering mass of white.

The air was thick with them. Their wings brushed hands, shoulders, faces. The markings on their wings swelled and glowed scarlet. They spat, and their poison burned where it fell.

Many people staggered, screaming in pain. Others dropped their weapons, covered their heads and began to run, heedlessly trampling the fallen ones in their panic.

Run, you ugly barefaces, Lief thought, watching in satisfaction. Leave us to ourselves!

With part of his mind he was aware that the clock was still striking.

Nine . . . ten . . .

Soon . . .

With a shock he felt himself thrown to the ground, held fast. Barda pinned his shoulders down. Then, horribly, he felt Jasmine's fingers tearing at his face.

'No!' he moaned. 'No—'

Jasmine loomed above him. She was breathing in great, sobbing gasps. Her brow was beaded with sweat, and tears were pouring down her cheeks. But her mouth was set in a hard, straight line.

Eleven . . .

He felt a searing pain. He heard Barda cursing. He heard himself screaming.

Then all was darkness.

10 - The Bees

Lief woke suddenly, his heart pounding with fear. There was a low ringing in his ears. Needles of pain stabbed at his face and neck.

The ringing sound slowly faded away.

I must have had a nightmare, Lief thought. He lay very still, calming himself. Shadows flitted at the edges of his mind, but he could remember no dream. What had woken him, then? Woken him in such terror?

Cautiously he tried opening his eyes. They felt swollen and tender, and he could only open them a little. Through his eyelashes he saw blue sky, and sunlight filtering through the leaves of a tree.

It was broad daylight!

He licked his dry lips and swallowed painfully. He realised that he was very thirsty.

He turned his head to look for his water flask. Pain flashed through him, bringing tears to his eyes.

Have I been burned? he thought in confusion. He could smell the ashes of a fire. He could see the remains of a small fire near the trunk of the tree, not far from where he lay.

He could see nothing else. No pack. No water flask. Only trampled earth, deeply rutted with the marks of wagon wheels.

Gritting his teeth, closing his mind to the pain, he turned his head to the other side.

Jasmine lay there, deeply asleep. Her cheek was pillowed on her arm. In her hand was the tiny jar of green ointment. It was as though she had been using the ointment just before she fell asleep.

She was wearing the blue clothes of a Masked Ones acrobat. Her hair was covered by a woollen cap. Her face was smeared with mud and what looked like blood.

Beyond her, as far as Lief could see, the field stretched broad and empty except for the ashes of an enormous fire. The fence had been broken down in several places.

What has happened to us? he thought wildly. Where is Barda? His heart began to thud.

Barda is in danger . . .

The feeling was strong, but another feeling, or vague memory, was mingling with it. Something about Kree . . .

A fly buzzed close to his face, then settled on his arm. Lief wanted to brush it away, but feared that he could not lift his hand.

Another fly joined the first. Then Lief realised that they were not flies at all, but bees.

And at the same moment, as if in a dream, he heard sounds drifting on the breeze from somewhere beyond the field. The jingling of tiny bells. And singing.

Here we are in Happy Vale,
Pretty bees, busy bees.
Three long hours on the trail,
Fuzzy, buzzy bees.

Did you hear the clock strike eight?
Clever bees, tired bees.
Pray that we are not too late,
Hungry, bumbly bees.

As if the song had thrown open a window in Lief's mind, he suddenly understood several things at once.

He had been woken by the striking of the Happy Vale clock. The sound had filled him with terror, but he did not know why.

It was eight o'clock in the morning. The Masked Ones had left in the night. He and Jasmine were alone here, with no weapons, no food, no water.

And the person passing by the field, the singer of the jolly little song, was . . .

Trust only old friends . . .

Lief tried to shout, but his voice was a husky croak. He struggled to sit up. His head swam and he nearly fell back. Grimly he propped himself up with his hands.

So it was that he saw the great black bird swooping towards him. He saw the swarm of bees stretching like a trail of smoke all the way to the field gate. And he saw a shabby caravan, drawn by a fat old horse and driven by a huge, brown-skinned, golden-haired man, turning into the gateway and following the line of bees.

On the side of the caravan was a familiar, faded sign.

'Jasmine!' Lief croaked.

Jasmine's eyes flew open in fright and widened even further when she saw Lief sitting up and looking at her.

'Lief?' she murmured uncertainly, scrambling to her knees. 'Are you—all right?'

He nodded, wincing at the pain in his neck. Why was Jasmine staring at him so strangely?

With a chill, he wondered what he looked like. He lifted his hand to his cheek.

Searing pain. Sticky cream coating his fingertips.

'Am I—burned?' he managed to croak.

Jasmine shook her head. She pulled off her cap, and her black hair tumbled around her shoulders. Her eyes were very dark. Filli was hiding beneath her jacket, only the tip of his nose visible.

'Do you not remember what happened last night?' Jasmine asked. 'What—what I did?'

'No.' Lief swallowed painfully.

She breathed a long sigh and closed her eyes as if in relief.

'Barda,' Lief rasped. 'Where is—?'

'He went in pursuit of the Masked Ones,' Jasmine whispered. 'Kree is with him. Lief—'

'At last!' boomed a voice. 'And both alive, by the looks of it!'

Jasmine jumped violently and swung around. She had been concentrating on Lief so intently that she had not even noticed the approaching caravan.

Kree flew to her, landing on her arm. She leaped to her feet.

'Steven!' she cried. 'Am I dreaming?'

Steven the pedlar's face split in a broad grin. 'Not unless I am dreaming as well,' he roared back. 'How fortunate that I was in these parts! I have been in Purley, with my mother's best hive of bees. We heard that flowers were blooming in the east, but I fear there are not yet enough to have made the journey worthwhile.'

He brought the horse to a halt beside them and

climbed down from the driver's seat.

'Steven, did you see some wagons on the road?' Jasmine asked feverishly. 'Wagons driven by people in masks?'

Steven nodded. 'Oh, yes, I met the Masked Ones,' he said. 'Traded with them, in fact, as I have often done before. They were far fewer than the last time we met—the inner circle only, and a few youngsters. Silent and nervous they were, too.'

He grinned. 'Later I met someone even more interesting—or found him, rather, thanks to Kree.'

Jasmine shrieked. Steven laughed, strode to the back of the caravan and threw open the doors.

'There he is,' he said triumphantly, as Jasmine jumped eagerly into the van. 'He was lying in a ditch—put to sleep by some Masked One trickery or other, no doubt. If Kree had not been guarding him, I would have passed him by.'

'Steven!' Lief rasped. 'Is it—Barda?'

Steven looked around and seemed to see him properly for the first time.

'Lief!' he gasped, dismayed. 'By the heavens! What happened to you?'

'I—am not quite sure,' said Lief, trying to smile.

Jasmine climbed back out of the caravan, her face very grave. Lief's heart seemed to leap into his throat.

'Surely Barda is not worse than I thought?' Steven asked anxiously.

Jasmine shook her head. 'He stirred when I spoke

to him,' she said. 'He took some water, and said a few words. I daresay the spell, or whatever it was, will pass off in time.'

Steven laughed with relief. 'Why, I thought from your expression that we would soon be attending his funeral!' he exclaimed.

Jasmine said nothing. Still she did not look at Lief. He had groaned with relief on hearing that Barda was safe. Now the tightness in his chest came back in force.

Steven glanced at him, then back at Jasmine.

'Cheer up, girl!' he said to her loudly, raising his bushy eyebrows. 'Your long face is worrying Lief half to death!'

Jasmine bit her lip, but still she did not look up, or speak.

Steven frowned at her. 'I did good trade with the Masked Ones, did I not?' he said, a little coldly. 'They wanted some Queen Bee honey. It is in short supply, but I agreed to give them six jars when I saw the goods they offered in exchange.'

'Our weapons and our packs,' Jasmine murmured. 'Yes—I saw them in the caravan. Our packs are still sealed, just as we left them.'

Lief stared at her in amazement. She sounded as if the return of all their possessions was of very little importance.

Steven's frown deepened. No doubt he had expected joy, or at least a word of thanks.

'I think the Masked Ones had forgotten they had

them,' he said. 'They found them in an empty wagon, when they were rummaging about looking for things to trade. Then the fox-faced woman remembered the weapons, and brought them out, too.'

'You recognised them?' asked Lief.

Steven shrugged. 'Of course!' he said. 'No-one could mistake your sword. I was astounded, and fearful, too, but I did not let the Masked Ones see. They said they had found your possessions by the side of the road. I doubted that was true, but it seemed unwise to challenge them. If they had fought me, Nevets would have killed them all.'

He grimaced as he spoke Nevets' name.

How strange it must be to carry your brother within you, Lief thought. Especially a brother who is your opposite. Who is a savage . . . a killer!

Steven eyed Lief and tugged his rough beard. 'I did not want the Masked Ones harmed, at the time,' he added. 'Perhaps I was wrong.'

'No,' Jasmine said in a low voice. 'The one who caused the trouble was already dead.'

She pressed her lips together. Plainly she was going to say no more.

Steven tugged at his beard even harder. 'They had thrown open every wagon in their search, so I was sure that you were not with them,' he muttered. 'But the wagons were all in confusion, as if they had been packed very hurriedly, for a quick departure.'

'So when they had gone, you followed their wagon

tracks back along the road,' Lief said. 'And so found Barda—'

'And Kree, who led me on to you,' Steven said.

He looked from Lief to Jasmine, and shook his head.

'How did this happen?' he burst out. 'How is it that I find you in this state? Why, the last I heard, you were travelling the kingdom in fine style, on horseback and escorted by troop of guards!'

'It is a long story,' Lief said. 'Steven, you must help us! We must move on. We must move on, towards the west.'

His mouth felt stiff. The pain in his face and neck stabbed at him mercilessly, and his dizziness had returned. He swayed.

Steven crouched beside him and took his arm. 'We are going nowhere today, Lief,' he said firmly. 'Later, when you are more recovered—'

'No!' Jasmine broke in. 'We must leave here now!'

Steven spun around. This time he was really scowling. His golden eyes darkened ominously, as if his savage brother Nevets was stirring within him.

'Are you mad, girl?' he snarled. 'Lief is not fit to travel! Look at him!'

Look at him!

Filli wailed, and Jasmine buried her face in her hands. Lief felt cold. Cold to his very bones.

Jasmine lifted her head. She looked directly at Lief.

'There is much to tell you,' she said in a low voice. 'But one thing I should have told you at once. It was cowardly of me not to do so, but then Steven came, with Barda, and I thought . . .'

You thought they would help you tell me, Lief thought. Tell me that, whatever it was that happened to me last night, my face will never . . .

He held Jasmine's eyes steadily, bracing himself for what was to come.

Jasmine wet her lips. 'Last night, all was confusion,' she said. 'There was panic, and screaming. People were running everywhere. You were in great pain, and not— not in your senses. It took Barda and I both to hold you down.'

Her voice trembled. She shook her head impatiently and went on.

'The ordinary people scattered—fled in every direction. The Masked Ones threw everything into the wagons and left the field at a gallop. It was only after they had gone, and you had calmed a little, that we realised—realised that the Belt—the Belt of Deltora—'

The Belt? Lief thought in confusion. What has this to do with . . .?

He put his hands to his waist.

The Belt of Deltora was gone.

11 - The Trail

When the village clock struck nine, Steven, Lief and Jasmine were still in the field. A small fire was crackling between them, and Steven was pouring hot tea into cups. He had refused to go in pursuit of the Masked Ones.

'They would not have touched the Belt,' he said firmly. 'To them, it is an evil thing. They learn to hate it from the cradle.'

'Why?' Lief said. He swallowed. His throat had been soothed by the Queen Bee honey Steven had given him, but it still felt raw.

He now knew the reason. It was because in the night, just before midnight, he had screamed in agony. Screamed, and screamed . . .

'Later, I will give you something that explains the Masked Ones a little,' said Steven, pushing a steaming cup into his hands. 'For now, forget them and think about the ordinary folk who were travelling with them.'

Lief sipped his tea, staring at the cloud of bees swarming on the fence at the far edge of the field. He let his mind drift, knowing that it was best not to force his memory.

Gradually, much of what had happened the night before had come back to him. But he remembered nothing from the moment the clock began to strike midnight. He knew only what Jasmine had told him.

It was horrifying, almost unbelievable, but he knew it was true. In the mirror Steven had brought from the caravan, he had seen the proof—the raw patches on his cheekbones, chin and neck, gleaming scarlet beneath their layers of sticky green cream.

He shuddered, thinking how narrow his escape had been. How nearly he had been a Masked One for life, the beautiful blue bird face bonded forever with his own. A few more seconds . . .

He reached for Jasmine's hand.

'No-one but Barda and I were with you at midnight, Lief,' she said in a low voice. 'The Belt must have been stolen before then—while you were wandering alone in the crowd. Though how it could have been taken without you noticing, I do not understand.'

Her words stirred a memory in Lief's mind. Bess, talking to Rust:

If he can take a purse from a man's coat, without that man noticing, he can learn to deceive an audience with ease.

'Zerry!' he exclaimed.

'Who?' asked Steven, leaning forward.

'The little thief?' Jasmine cried at the same moment. 'Of course! But Lief, how—?'

'Some children jostled me in the field,' Lief said slowly. 'I remember now. Zerry was one of them. He must have taken the Belt then.'

He stared across the field, remembering.

'Before that, I was feeling—confused,' he said. 'The Belt's magic, and the magic of the mask, were battling within me, I am sure of it. One minute I would think I was a Masked One. The next minute a voice inside me would remind me I was not. And I could not stop shivering. But after I was jostled by the children, all that disappeared.'

'Because the Belt had gone,' murmured Jasmine.

Lief nodded. Absently, he noticed that the bees had risen from the fence. Now they were swarming back towards the road in a ragged stream.

He focused on them. He stared.

'Zerry must have known exactly what he was after,' Steven said thoughtfully. 'An ordinary thief would have searched your pockets. That can only mean that, child or not, he is an ally of the guardian of the north—a servant of the Shadow Lord.'

Jasmine swallowed the last of her tea and jumped up. 'We can still catch him! He is on foot. No doubt he escaped from the field last night with everyone else— and went by the road, for fear of becoming lost.'

'But which way did he go?' Steven asked, tossing

dust on the fire to put it out. 'Among the mass of tracks, how are we to find those of one small boy?'

'Look at the bees!' Lief said.

Steven glanced at him in surprise, then looked to where he was pointing.

A dark cloud of bees was swirling over the dust of the road.

'What are they doing?' Steven growled. 'There is nothing for them out there!'

'Oh, but there is!' Lief could not help smiling, despite the stinging pain in his face.

'Yesterday, Zerry stole honey from the store wagon,' he said. 'He must have hidden himself away and had a secret feast. When he jostled me last night, his hands were sticky with honey—and no doubt it had dripped on his clothes and shoes as well. Look! The bees can smell it!'

They were all on their feet now, shading their eyes, staring at the bees. The swarm was slowly moving west.

'You see?' Lief said softly. 'The bees are following a honey trail. To find Zerry, and the Belt, all we have to do is to follow them!'

✳

Lief rode inside the caravan so that his injuries would be protected from the dust of the road. He rolled up his cloak for a pillow and tried to sleep, like Barda, but sleep would not come.

Long hours passed. Then his heart leaped as he heard Steven calling the horse to a halt.

'Why have we stopped?' he asked anxiously, as Jasmine threw open the caravan doors with Filli chattering on her shoulder. 'Is Zerry—?'

'The bees have lost the trail,' Jasmine answered flatly.

As Lief clambered to the ground, he saw that the road no longer ran between open fields. Now it was overshadowed on both sides by tall rocks and trees with pale, thin branches that clattered together like bones.

He walked with Jasmine to the front of the van, where Steven was pouring water into a bucket for his thirsty horse.

Immediately ahead, there was a road leading off to the left. It was marked by a signpost so faded that Lief could not see what it said.

Kree was perched on the signpost. The bees were swarming uncertainly behind it, where there was a large clearing. Wheel tracks criss-crossed the open space, leading off in both directions.

Lief approached the signpost, and looked at it.

Something stirred in his mind. He felt he had seen that name somewhere else, not long ago. But where?

'The boy met a wagon here, it seems,' Steven said,

moving up behind him with Jasmine. 'And surely not by chance. We can follow—but which way?'

'The trees here can tell me nothing,' Jasmine said grimly. 'They are weak and ill—barely alive. The wheel tracks tell a story, however. Only one wagon moved west. And by the deep grooves it left behind, it had been standing here for a day or two before that.'

'Indeed,' Steven nodded, peering at the tracks. 'All the other wagons came and went quite quickly. And they all went south to Riverdale. No doubt the boy is with one of those.'

'I cannot see how a meeting was arranged,' Lief frowned. 'Zerry was travelling all day yesterday. And Happy Vale was deserted. How was the message passed?'

'You might as well ask how Zerry knew he must steal the Belt,' Jasmine said impatiently. 'Perhaps he saw it written in the sky! Perhaps the clouds formed letters saying, "Steal the Belt of Deltora. Meet at the Riverdale signpost"! What does it matter?'

Lief's heart jolted. He had just remembered where he had seen the name 'Riverdale' before! And with the memory had come a vivid picture—and an idea. A wild idea . . .

'It might matter a great deal,' he exclaimed, kneeling and fumbling in his pocket for paper and pencil. 'Remember the Happy Vale noticeboard? Everyone in the troupe saw that as we moved through the town. Did you, Steven?'

'Of course,' Steven said gravely.

Lief put the paper on the ground in front of him. 'The main notice is not important,' he said. 'But I want you both to help me remember all the small ones. Word for word, if possible.'

'I did not read them all,' murmured Jasmine, flushing a little. She still felt awkward because she read so slowly.

'You may not read fast, Jasmine, but you observe without even trying,' said Lief. 'That will be your part— and the most important one, if I am right.'

Quickly they finished the first notice, and the second. Jasmine could help no further after that, but Steven and Lief soon worked out the next three between them.

'I cannot help you on the last one,' Steven said. 'It concerned that villain Laughing Jack, the moneylender. I did not read it.'

'It does not matter,' Lief said. 'I remember it. I noticed it particularly, because the first words —"Seek the Nomad"—were odd.'

'Ah, yes,' said Steven sourly. 'Laughing Jack is a great one for eye-catching notices. And he is a nomad, for he has no fixed home. He appears without warning outside one town or another, and in between it is as if he vanishes. Where was he camped this time?'

'Here,' Lief said, writing out the last notice and drawing a border around it. 'At the Riverdale signpost!'

12 - The Chase

J asmine exclaimed with interest, and craned her neck to see the words Lief had written. But Steven's frown had become a scowl.

'Ah!' he said in disgust. 'So now we know whose wagon stayed so long! Laughing Jack never leaves a place until he has wrung it dry.'

He shook his head. 'No doubt most of the other tracks were made by the poor fools who came to do business with him.'

'What is so wrong about lending money?' Jasmine asked, puzzled.

Steven snorted. 'Nothing, if it is done fairly,' he said. 'But Laughing Jack preys on those who are desperate.'

He saw that his companions did not understand him, and raised his voice slightly as he explained.

'Laughing Jack lends his victims what they ask, or more, and makes them sign a paper that half of them cannot even read,' he said. 'A season or two later he returns, demanding that the loan be repaid.'

He paused. Dark shadows flickered in his golden eyes.

'And then?' Jasmine prompted.

Steven's fists clenched.

'And then his victims discover that they have sworn to pay back ten or twenty times as much as they borrowed,' he muttered. 'If they do not pay, which most often they cannot, Laughing Jack takes possession of their homes, their beasts, their furniture—everything they own.'

'I have not heard of this!' Lief exclaimed.

Steven shrugged. 'Laughing Jack has been a plague in the land for years without number, and dark rumours have gathered about him. His victims are too afraid to complain to anyone in authority.'

'Afraid?' Lief murmured.

Steven grimaced. 'He is an evil man, and when they have given him all they have, and it is still not enough, what else can he take from them, but their lives?'

As his companions exclaimed in horror, he shook his head.

'I am wasting our time by speaking of things that we cannot change at present,' he said gruffly. 'Lief, what are we to do now?'

Lief spread his paper out before them on the ground. He had drawn borders around all the notices, shaping them as he remembered.

'Now it is your turn to test your memory, Jasmine,' he said. 'See the Happy Vale board in your mind. All the notices were pinned into place, were they not?'

Jasmine nodded. 'Pinned untidily, too,' she said. 'The people who put them up had taken little care.'

'I think they took a great deal of care,' Lief said.

As she raised her eyebrows in surprise, he gave her the pencil. 'See if you can remember where the pins were placed on each notice,' he said. 'Mark the places with a dot.'

He crossed his fingers for luck as Jasmine bent over the paper and began to mark it.

She finished the first notice, and then the second. Now and then she would close her eyes, as if seeing a picture in her mind, before going on.

By the time she had finished marking the third notice, Lief knew he had been right.

He glanced at Steven. The big man's eyes were bulging with astonishment. He seemed about to speak, but Lief shook his head warningly. He did not want Jasmine's concentration to be disturbed.

Jasmine moved on with increasing speed. In moments the work was done. She threw down the pencil and pushed the paper away.

'There,' she muttered. 'I have done it. Though I cannot see why—'

She glanced up and saw their faces.

'What is it?' she asked blankly, looking down at the paper again.

Dean the Smoke
will trade 3
hens for a
Sack of Grain

For Sale
These are bargains!
Fine bed. Table with
2 chairs   Kate
          Mend-shoe

Dame Henstoke
can teach you to
dance. Cheap Ra

Hank Modestee, who
can follow orders, needs
work. Ask at tavern.

If you want
to send goods
ahead to Purley
see Andos the meek

Seek the Nomad! Laughing Jack
your friendly travelling moneylender,
is now camped at the
Riverdale signpost.

'Read the words beneath the dots aloud,' said Lief grimly. 'Read them in order.'

Shaking her head, Jasmine began to do as he asked. 'The ... three ... are ... with ... you ...' she read, and caught her breath.

'Go on!' Lief urged.

'Follow orders,' Jasmine went on, her voice rising. 'Send goods ... to ... Laughing Jack ... at Riverdale signpost.'

'And that was how it was done,' Steven exclaimed, slapping his knee. 'The simple cunning of it! A message in plain sight, but perfectly disguised. "The three are with you. Follow orders. Send goods to Laughing Jack, at Riverdale signpost."'

Lief was only half listening. He was staring at the paper.

Something about it was still nagging at him. But what? The hidden message had been revealed. What further secrets could the notices hold?

'The "three" are you two and Barda, of course,' Steven went on excitedly. 'The "orders" must be Zerry's standing orders to steal the Belt of Deltora if you crossed his path. The "goods" are the Belt itself.'

He shook his head. 'This guardian of the north must be well organised indeed, with a secret network of allies who go about their usual business unless and until they are needed. Zerry was used because he was with the Masked Ones. Laughing Jack was used because he was plying his evil trade in the north. No doubt he himself put the notices on the board just before you arrived.'

'But how did the guardian learn that we were with the Masked Ones in the first place?' Jasmine frowned.

Steven was not interested in more mysteries. The one that had already been solved was enough for him.

'So Laughing Jack is in league with the Enemy,' he muttered. 'Why does that not surprise me?'

Abruptly he turned and strode towards the caravan.

'Let us be on our way,' he called over his shoulder. 'We must make haste. Our quarry's wagon, I hear, is as fast as the wind.'

'Then we will never catch him!' Jasmine cried anxiously, scrambling to her feet.

Steven reached the van, jumped up to the driver's seat, and began fossicking in a sack crushed into one corner.

'Certainly we will,' he said, without looking up. 'I have a trick or two up my sleeve.'

He pulled a small green bottle from the sack, and nodded with satisfaction.

By the time Lief and Jasmine reached him, he had climbed down and was whispering in the horse's ear. The horse snorted eagerly and whisked her tail.

Steven smiled. 'I am looking forward to this,' he said softly. 'My brother and I have long wanted to meet Laughing Jack.'

He opened the green bottle and emptied it into the horse's bucket. The unmistakable apple smell of Queen Bee cider filled the air. The horse plunged its nose into the bucket and drank eagerly.

'Your horse drinks Queen Bee cider?' Jasmine asked in astonishment.

Steven was removing the strings of bells attached to the reins. 'Only on special occasions,' he said. 'And, of course, Mellow is no ordinary horse.'

Lief and Jasmine glanced at one another. Mellow certainly looked ordinary. Very ordinary indeed.

As if she knew what they were thinking, Mellow pawed the ground. She had nearly finished the cider in the bucket. They could hear the sound of her tongue rasping on the metal sides as she licked up the last few drops.

'I would climb into the van at once, if I were you,' Steven said quickly. 'Make sure the doors are locked.'

'Steven, I think that Jasmine, at least, should ride with you,' Lief objected.

Steven smiled without humour. 'She would be very sorry if she did,' he said.

Mellow raised her head. She bared her long, yellow teeth and neighed.

Every bee in the clearing seemed to stop in mid air. Then the swarm rose in a black cloud. Kree squawked, and soared high into the sky.

'Make haste!' Steve said urgently. He snatched up the bucket, threw the empty bottle and the bells inside it and swung himself up to the driver's seat.

Lief and Jasmine ran to the back of the caravan. Jasmine jumped in. Lief was about to follow when

Mellow neighed again. He looked around, and the hair rose on the back of his neck.

The swarm was upon them. The horse's head and neck seethed with bees. The reins were heavy with bees. And like a thick, black carpet unrolling, bees were swarming back, back, towards the van.

'Shut the doors!' bellowed Steven.

His heart beating wildly, Lief leaped into the van and slammed the doors behind him. In moments the dimness had became darkness, and the walls and roof were vibrating with frenzied humming.

'The bees,' Jasmine whispered.

And then they were moving. Slowly at first. Then faster, faster, faster—until all Lief and Jasmine could hear were the faint, clicking sounds of hoofs that seemed barely to touch the ground, and the wild humming of the bees.

13 - The Funnel

On they raced, the caravan smoothly rocking, its timbers creaking gently. Jasmine put more green cream on Lief's face, and the stinging pain eased a little. They ate traveller's biscuits and a little dried fish, washed down with water from their flasks.

After a time, Barda woke. He was confused and full of questions. Jasmine began telling him of all that had happened. And, incredibly, in the middle of the story, Lief fell asleep.

He woke knowing that something had changed. He could hear a muffled roaring sound, but it was not the humming of the bees. The gentle rocking had ceased.

'We have stopped,' Jasmine's voice whispered.

Lief turned his head and saw her beside him, just a shape in the dimness. Filli was sitting on her shoulder nibbling a fragment of biscuit.

'How long have I been asleep?' Lief exclaimed, sitting up.

'I do not know,' Jasmine said. 'I slept, too.'

The doors of the caravan creaked open. Cold white light flooded in. Moonlight.

Steven's face appeared in the doorway, his finger pressed warningly to his lips.

'We have travelled far,' he whispered. 'We are in a valley in the foothills of the mountains. Laughing Jack's wagon turned in to a side path not far ahead. It seems he has stopped for the night. How is Barda?'

'Asleep again,' Jasmine answered. 'I gave him more honey. Filli will watch over him, and come for us if he needs us.'

Steven nodded, and beckoned.

Filli sprang nimbly from Jasmine's shoulder and importantly took his place by Barda's side. Lief caught up his cloak and his sword and followed Jasmine out into the night.

The moon sailed overhead in a sea of stars. It was almost as bright as day, but everything was black, white and grey. There were no trees. The mountains glowered above them, black as the sky. Rocks rose all around them, glistening in the moonlight. A dull roaring filled the air.

'Waterfall,' Steven breathed.

He led the way to the front of the van. Mellow stood there, placidly munching leaves from a scraggy bush. She had never looked more ordinary. There was not a bee to be seen.

'Where is Kree?' Jasmine asked, looking around in sudden alarm.

'Far behind, I fear,' Steven whispered. 'He could not keep up with us.'

Mellow snickered, as if with satisfaction, and tore off another leaf.

Steven grinned. 'Come on—and quietly,' he said. 'This villain is slippery. We must take him by surprise.'

A few steps ahead, a path led up a gentle rise. Beyond the rise they could see the waterfall—a broad, foaming sheet of white, covering the cliff like a veil.

A wooden gate had once barred the path, but this had been pushed down and now lay flat on the ground. The sign fixed to it had been trampled by hoofs, but the words could still be read.

Quietly the companions moved over the gate. As soon as his foot touched the path, Lief's body began to tingle. The Belt was somewhere ahead. He could feel it. He began to move faster.

'Why would such a beautiful thing have an ugly name like "The Funnel"?' Jasmine whispered, looking up to where the waterfall began, high above them.

'That question will be answered when we see the bottom, I fear,' Lief muttered.

In moments he was proved right. They reached the top of the rise. The waterfall thundered directly ahead. And below . . .

They stared, awe-struck.

Below them, at the base of the waterfall, yawned the foaming mouth of The Funnel.

It was if the jaws of the earth had opened to receive the great flood of water pouring from the clifftop. Deep within the vast basin of rock the water was spinning like a gigantic whirlpool, swirling down into The Funnel's throat like water rushing down a drain.

'A pleasant place to spend the night, indeed,' Steven muttered.

Lief tore his eyes away from The Funnel and scanned the gently sloping rock that surrounded it.

At first he could see nothing but gleams and shadows. Then, suddenly, there was a tiny movement. His eyes focused, and he jumped.

Where before he had seen only bare rock and a mist of spray from the waterfall, he now saw four black horses yoked to a large wagon. A thin man was standing in front of the horses, a brimming bucket in his hand.

'I thought so,' Steven breathed. 'His wagon is protected by disguising magic. Like your cloak, Lief, though far more powerful. That is how he comes and goes unseen. The Enemy has given him some powers in return for service, it seems. We will have to take care.'

'I cannot see Zerry,' Lief whispered. 'He must be asleep in the back of the wagon.'

Cautiously, keeping low, they began to follow the path down.

They reached the valley floor and hid behind a boulder. Laughing Jack was still standing with his horses. They could not see his face, but they could see the bucket swinging in his bony hand, and hear his high, grating voice.

'Would you like a little water, you stupid beasts?' he was saying. 'Ah yes, of course you would. You have not drunk all day. You must be thirsty. Very, very thirsty. So—will I give you a drink?'

The horses stretched out their necks and seemed to groan.

'He is tormenting them!' breathed Jasmine. She was trembling with fury.

'Look!' cried Laughing Jack, swinging the bucket even more so that water slopped over the sides and onto the ground. 'Water! Can you see it? Can you smell it? Well, you cannot have it!'

Cackling with laughter, he turned away from the horses and moved into view, still carrying the brimming bucket.

Lief stared at him with loathing. He was dressed in black from head to foot. A braid of greasy brown hair hung down his back, skinny as a rat's tail. His face was skull-like. Skin like old leather stretched tightly across his jutting bones, and the large teeth gleamed in a permanent grin.

A little distance from the wagon, Laughing Jack had made comfortable arrangements for his evening meal.

Bread, fruit, cheese and some sort of sausage lay on a platter near a small camping stove. A plump red sack had been placed in front of the platter, for a seat. All of this was protected from the spray of the waterfall by a huge red and white striped umbrella.

No doubt that umbrella once stood over the market stall of one of his victims, Lief thought.

He realised that his fists were clenched, and forced himself to relax. The important thing now was to find the Belt. Everything else had to wait.

Laughing Jack filled a kettle from the bucket. He lit the stove and set the kettle upon the flames. Then he sat down with a satisfied sigh, and helped himself to bread and sausage.

'He can still see the wagon,' Jasmine whispered. 'We will never get to it unseen, even under Lief's cloak.'

'You will if I will distract him,' Steven answered.

Alerted by the grim tone of his voice, Lief glanced at him uneasily. Dark shadows were moving in the golden eyes. Steven's brother, Nevets, was very aware of what was happening.

My brother and I have long looked forward to meeting Laughing Jack . . .

'Steven, take care,' he pleaded. 'Before—before anything else happens, I must find the Belt.'

Steven gritted his teeth. 'I know that,' he said.

He stepped out from behind the rock, put his hands in his pockets and walked casually forward.

'Good evening, sir!' he called. 'A fine night, is it not?'

Laughing Jack stiffened. Slowly he turned his head.

'Did I startle you?' Steven said cheerily, strolling towards him. 'I beg your pardon. I thought you had surely heard me coming, but the waterfall is very noisy, of course.'

Laughing Jack made no reply.

Steven paced admiringly around the striped umbrella. 'Why, you are set up very nicely here!' he exclaimed. 'May I join you?'

He sat down on the other side of the stove. Laughing Jack was forced to turn away from the wagon to keep him in view.

'Now,' Lief breathed.

He drew Jasmine close to him and wrapped her in his cloak. Together they began to creep towards the wagon.

'This waterfall is a fine sight indeed,' Steven said. 'It takes my mind from my troubles.'

'Troubles?' murmured Laughing Jack, leaning forward slightly.

'Indeed,' Steven sighed. 'The cart I use to take my goods to market is quite worn out, and I have no gold to buy another. People say I should sell the jewels my old aunt left me. But I do not want to do that. They have been in my family for generations.'

'Ah!' Laughing Jack leaned forward even further. 'Well, well. What a fortunate chance that we met. I may be able to help you.'

Lief smiled wryly. Steven had all the moneylender's attention now. No doubt Laughing Jack thought he had found a perfect victim.

The horses did not look around as Lief and Jasmine approached. Blinkers shielded their eyes, and their heads hung low. Straining against their heavy harness, they were trying to lick water from the rock.

Lief's heart ached for them. After this is over, we will help you, he promised them silently.

As though he had spoken aloud, one of the horses on the far side lifted its head. Fearful that it would make a sound, Lief tightened his grip on Jasmine and slipped quickly around to the back of the wagon.

He eased the door open, hoping against hope that it would not creak.

Steven and Laughing Jack were still talking.

'There is nothing I like better than helping those less fortunate than myself,' Laughing Jack was saying. 'Why, I *live* to do good. And you seem such a worthy fellow. Let me lend you the money for your cart! How much do you need? Twenty gold coins? Fifty?'

'Fifty!' Steven exclaimed. 'Why, with fifty I could put a new roof on the house as well!'

'All the better!' cried Laughing Jack. And Lief could almost see his skull's grin broadening.

The cart door was now fully open. Lief and Jasmine looked inside.

A mattress covered by a glorious patchwork quilt took up most of the floor space. Around the walls, baskets of food and valuable objects of all kinds were stacked to the roof. An empty honey jar had rolled into the corner nearest the door.

But there was no sign of Zerry.

'Where is he?' Jasmine breathed.

Lief shook his head helplessly.

Zerry was not in the cart. And he knew that the Belt was not there either. If it was, he would feel it.

He began to close the cart door. As he did, a scrap of paper fluttered from a fold in the quilt and landed on the floor. Jasmine picked it up and glanced at it. Her eyes widened in horror.

She thrust the note at Lief.

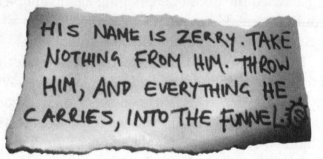

HIS NAME IS ZERRY. TAKE NOTHING FROM HIM. THROW HIM, AND EVERYTHING HE CARRIES, INTO THE FUNNEL.

14 - Choices

Understanding broke over Lief in a wave of burning heat. He stumbled away from the wagon, hardly knowing what he did. He heard Jasmine gasp out his name, but he did not turn. He could not face the horror in her eyes.

The Belt was gone—gone with Zerry, down, down into the terrible throat of The Funnel. Perhaps only minutes before they arrived.

That is why I can still feel it, he thought. That is why I was so sure . . .

Blindly he stared at the thundering waterfall, the greedy, swirling water beneath.

Zerry, whatever he had been promised, had only been a puppet—a puppet used ruthlessly by people far more powerful, far more wicked, than himself.

He had just been someone who could steal the Belt. Someone who could carry it safely, as a true servant of the Shadow Lord could not.

Someone who could be disposed of as easily as a scrap of paper or an empty honey jar.

'So,' Laughing Jack was saying loudly. 'All you have to do is sign this paper, my good fellow, and your troubles are over.'

Slowly Lief turned his head to look at the evil man who could kill a boy, amuse himself by tormenting his horses, then calmly sit down to eat his dinner.

Laughing Jack was holding a piece of parchment in one hand and a small money bag in the other. He shook the bag. The coins inside jingled invitingly.

'I fear I am not much of a one for reading,' Steven said, staring blankly at the paper.

'Oh, this is nothing!' The thin man flapped the parchment casually. 'Just a few words saying that Laughing Jack lent you fifty gold coins. It proves you came by the money honestly, do you see? You would not like anyone to think you had stolen it, would you?'

'No indeed!' Steven said earnestly.

'Excellent!' said Laughing Jack. 'Now, I think I have a pen here . . .'

He put the parchment on his knee, and bent to look inside his coat.

Instantly Steven glanced up. He saw Lief standing staring at him, and his eyes seemed to flash. Immediately he looked back to Laughing Jack, his teeth bared in a savage grin.

Too late, Lief realised that he had given no sign of

what had happened. Steven thought they had found the Belt, and that now he could deal with Laughing Jack.

The moneylender had brought out a large pen and a bottle of black ink. Carefully he took the lid from the bottle, and dipped the pen into it.

'Now,' he said, his hand hovering over the parchment. 'Your name?'

Steven's grin broadened. 'Hank Modestee,' he said softly.

Laughing Jack grew very still.

'Ah—you have heard my name before, I see,' Steven said, still in that same, dangerously quiet voice. 'Perhaps you have also heard of my aunt—Dame Henstoke?'

'Who are you?' Laughing Jack hissed.

The next instant, his long legs were kicking out, and the stove and the kettle were crashing onto his enemy.

Pen, paper and ink bottle went flying as he sprang to his feet. He kicked the red bag he had been using as a seat, sending it rolling towards The Funnel. Then he bent double and scuttled towards the wagon like a great, lanky, four-legged spider, so fast that he seemed a blur.

Steven growled ferociously, thrusting the stove and kettle aside. His eyes were flashing gold to brown, brown to gold. His body was quivering . . .

And the plump red bag was tumbling down the sloping rock towards the raging water.

Lief shouted and hurled himself forward. Suddenly he knew what was in the bag. Knew why Laughing Jack had kicked it before he fled.

The bag had reached the edge of the rock. It was tipping . . .

Lief dived for it. His arms and chest hit the rock. His hands caught the last corner of the bag just as it slid over the lip of The Funnel. He held on with all his strength.

'Jasmine! Steven! Help me!' he shouted, twisting his neck, searching for a sign of them. But he could only see Laughing Jack, standing on the driver's seat of the wagon, a long whip in his hand. Jack's hollow eyes were blazing as he stared at something beyond Lief's vision.

The bag swung over the greedy, spinning water, drenched with spray. It was moving now. Someone inside it was struggling and kicking. Grimly Lief held on, his arms straining. He felt himself beginning to slide forward.

Desperately he dug the toes of his boots into the slippery rock, trying to hold himself back. But little by little the weight of the bag was pulling him after it.

He heard Jasmine cry out, and moments later felt her fling herself down behind him, felt her gripping his ankles.

Her strength was not enough—not enough, with the red bag dragging him down. The only way to save himself was to let go. But he could not let go.

'Steven!' he heard Jasmine scream over the thundering of the water.

Lief's head and shoulders were over the edge now. Spray beat on his face, filling his eyes and his nose. He gritted his teeth, held his breath . . .

And then, miraculously, he felt hands gripping him around the waist, lifting him back. Still he clung to the sodden, bulging bag, though his arms felt as if they were being pulled from their sockets, and his fingers were numb.

With joy he saw the bag rise, dripping, over the edge of The Funnel, and Steven's great arm reach out to gather it in. But still he did not release his grip.

Only when he was sprawled on higher ground, and the bag was safe, did he allow his fingers to be prised away from it. He lay back, trembling all over, as Jasmine cut the knots that held the bag closed.

Out rolled a squirming shape tied up like a parcel in a thick brown rug. Muffled shrieks reached their ears.

'Hold him, Steven!' Jasmine said sharply. She cut through the ropes and peeled the sodden rug aside. And there was Zerry, drenched, screaming and kicking.

Grimly Steven held him down.

'Let me go!' Zerry screeched, twisting violently. The buttons tore from his skimpy jacket. The ragged shirt beneath it ripped like paper.

And beneath the shirt, something gleamed. Something bright was looped around Zerry's neck, hanging down over his chest like a giant necklace.

Lief reached out. The moment he touched it, the Belt of Deltora fell into his hands. Tingling warmth flowed through him as he clasped it around his waist.

He closed his eyes, dazed with relief.

It is safe. It is with me. Safe . . .

The roaring of the waterfall was throbbing in his ears. It seemed to be echoing. Louder, louder . . . how could it be so loud?

Lief opened his eyes.

The waterfall was filled with stars—stars twinkling on a bed of midnight blue. It was as though, by some miraculous trick of the light, the night sky was reflected in the foaming, falling water.

And then the reflection seemed to rush forward. Something burst through the veil of the waterfall, through the clouds of spray—something real, and gigantic.

Roaring, it hovered over The Funnel, its scales sparkling in the moonlight. Its mighty wings were like dark blue velvet pierced with light. Its eyes shone like stars. Every one of its claws was like a new moon, curved and gleaming.

Zerry screamed in terror. He rolled over and covered his eyes. Jasmine, and even Steven, shrank back.

But Lief crawled to his feet and stood with his head up, his hands on the Belt of Deltora, his heart beating wildly. So—the waterfall veils a great cavern in the cliff, he thought, steadying himself. A safe hiding place, indeed, for—

'Greetings, king of Deltora!' thundered the dragon. 'At last you have come!'

'Greetings, dragon of the lapis-lazuli,' said Lief awkwardly. 'I—I came when I could.'

The dragon swept gracefully to shore. As it settled on the rock, not far away from the companions, Lief realised that, despite its enormous size, it was smaller than the other dragons he had seen. Smaller, and more delicate-looking.

The dragon looked at Lief closely. 'You are wet, and the poor, thin hide of your face is torn!' it accused, shaking its own dripping wings. 'What has befallen you, in this land of good fortune?'

Its gleaming eyes fell on Zerry. 'This boy is one of mine!' it growled. 'I can smell it! Did he dare to do you ill, king? Shall I deal with him?'

Zerry wailed and clutched Steven's arm. 'I did not mean it!' he gabbled. 'I did not know! Fern said the Belt was of no value—just part of a Masked Ones' costume, that Bess had given Lewin for himself.'

He wiped his nose on the sleeve of his jacket. 'She said I should steal it if I could. She said there was a man at the Riverdale turnoff who fancied it, and would pay well for it. She said it was my chance to get away from old Plug and her lessons, and go home to Rithmere with gold in my pocket. She wrote a note for me to give the man, but he—'

'The note said you were to be killed, you young fool!' Steven growled. 'If you had let Plug teach you to read, instead of spending all your time idling and thieving, you would have known that.'

'This boy of Rithmere laid hands on the Belt of Deltora?' thundered the dragon, baring its fangs.

'The boy is not our enemy,' Lief said quickly. 'Our enemy is—'

And for the first time since he shouted for help at the lip of The Funnel, he remembered Laughing Jack. The dragon was sitting where the wagon had been. He looked quickly at Steven.

'I had to force Nevets back, so I could come to your aid,' Steven said. 'Nevets and I cannot be long apart. We fight together or not at all. So Laughing Jack escaped. While I was still lifting you from The Funnel, he was up the hill and away. We will never catch him, or his poor beasts, now.'

Jasmine looked stricken.

Lief swallowed. 'Could not Mellow and the bees give chase and—?'

'They cannot work their magic again so soon,' Steven sighed. 'No—this time Laughing Jack has escaped the fate he deserves. But there will be another time. We will not forget.'

The dragon smacked its lips loudly, as if annoyed at being ignored.

'I am famished,' it announced. 'If you will excuse me, king, I will go and fill my belly.'

'You will not take humans, or their beasts, I hope!' Lief exclaimed, suddenly fearful.

'Unless you see a thin man driving four black horses,' growled Steven. 'You are very welcome to him.'

The dragon looked down its nose at them. 'Do you take me for a savage?' it demanded. 'Whatever dragons of other lands may stoop to, the dragons of the lapis-lazuli would never dine on warm blood. Ugh!'

It shuddered at the very thought.

'I beg your pardon,' Lief said hastily. 'But you will find little to satisfy your hunger, I fear. The land is poorly.'

'I have sensed that already, king,' the dragon growled, delicately smoothing the scales of its chest with one slender claw. 'It seems that the Enemy took advantage of my sleep.'

'He took advantage of all the dragons' sleep,' Lief said. 'The evil thing that is poisoning your territory is called the Sister of the North. My companions and I are journeying to find and destroy it.'

'Excellent!' the dragon exclaimed, inspecting its claws one by one. 'Before we leave, I will snatch a hasty meal in the Shifting Sands. It is not far, as the dragon flies, and no doubt Sand Beasts still thrive there. Ah, I well remember how they crunch between the teeth. Delightful!'

Lief exchanged glances with Jasmine and Steven. He cleared his throat.

'I fear you cannot come with us to find the Sister of the North,' he said. 'It is deep in the territory of the emerald, in a place called Shadowgate.'

The dragon seemed to frown. 'Indeed?' it said. 'We are very near the emerald border here, as it happens. But surely it will still take you quite a time to reach this Shadowgate?'

'Yes, it will,' Lief admitted ruefully.

The dragon was still looking at its claws. 'Certainly, before I slept, I promised not to stray from my own territory,' it murmured. 'But surely Dragonfriend did not mean this to prevent me from aiding the king who awoke me.'

It looked up, straight into Lief's eyes. 'Especially if the king should *ask* me to aid him,' it added.

Lief's heart gave a great thump. 'You would carry us to Shadowgate?' he asked. 'But what of the emerald dragon?'

'What of it?' The lapis-lazuli dragon yawned. 'It may be dead, for all we know. Its territory was infested with the Enemy's creatures. Any one of them would have destroyed it, if they found it sleeping.'

It sounded quite pleased at the thought.

'So,' it went on, its eyes sparkling. 'Good fortune brought us together, king. And you should never turn your back on your luck. Do you ask me to break my vow, and take you to Shadowgate?'

Lief took a deep breath. 'Yes,' he said. 'I do.'

15 – The Pass

And so, for the second time, Lief, Barda and Jasmine flew with a dragon. But this time was very different from the first.

It was not just that this time they were flying with a dragon who sang merrily as it flew. Or that this dragon seemed to glide through the air like a shooting star, with barely a beat of its wings.

It was not just that this dragon knew exactly where it was going because, unlike the dragon of the ruby, it prided itself on having learned about maps from the man it called Dragonfriend.

It was because, this time, they were not beginning a journey, but hurtling towards a journey's end. Mingled with their thoughts about what might be ahead were their thoughts of what had passed—thoughts they did not wish to share.

Barda was cursing himself for allowing the Masked

131

Ones to overpower him, when he caught up with them on the road to Purley. As a result of that failure, he had been useless to his companions just when they needed him most.

He scowled as he remembered waking in the caravan, with no idea where he was or what was happening. Kree had just arrived, and was screeching angrily at Steven's horse. Filli was chattering in his ear. His companions were nowhere to be seen. He had gone in search of them, but by the time he reached the waterfall, all the excitement was over.

Steven had filled his place admirably, of course. Without Steven, the quest would have ended in disaster.

But now, thought Barda, Steven is back in the caravan with Zerry and I am flying to Shadowgate. All is as it should be. I will not fail again.

Jasmine was thinking of the horses yoked to Laughing Jack's wagon. She was bitterly regretting that she had not been able to release them.

She had tried. If she had had more time, she could have done it. But Lief had called and she had run to him, leaving the horses to their fate.

Should she tell her companions the terrible thing that she had discovered as she followed Lief past the wagon after their fruitless effort to find the Belt?

No, she thought, hugging Filli and Kree closer, drawing comfort from their warmth. I must keep it to myself. Why grieve Lief and Barda to no purpose? Nothing can be done about it now.

Lief was fighting waking nightmares.

Again and again he relived the moment when the mask of Bede's adulthood settled over his face. Again and again he saw the Happy Vale noticeboard, its sad main message surrounded by the notes that Laughing Jack had left for Fern.

Again and again he saw the dread black shape rising above Otto's wagon, the green gleam that was its face, the smooth white fingers oozing back into its robes. Again and again he saw the Shadow Lord's brand burning on Fern's tortured face, and heard those last, whispered words.

Beware the Masked One . . .

He shook his head. Why could he not clear his mind of these things? They were in the past, and could not harm him now.

Bess was dead. Fern was dead. Laughing Jack had fled. And whoever had conjured up the deadly phantom was in the camp of the Masked Ones, far away. Further away every moment, as the lapis-lazuli dragon sped through the dawn, following the line of the mountains towards their goal.

But instead of fading, the visions were growing brighter. The feeling of something left undone, something not understood, was strengthening. The whispered warning was hissing more loudly in his ears.

Beware the Masked One . . .

And now another sound was mingling with the memory of Fern's dying breath. A faint, ringing tune—

four notes, repeated again and again, like a bird call, or the chiming of bells.

The Happy Vale clock, no doubt, Lief thought. The chime that comes before the striking of the hour.

His skin prickled, and he shut the sweet notes out of his mind. But always they returned, calling him.

✳

The sky was still dark when the dragon landed, in a dreary place of rock and dead, twisted trees.

The mountains rose all around them, black and brutal, capped with snow. Thick grey clouds smothered the rising sun. A chill wind moaned through the cliffs, bringing with it the howls of distant beasts.

Lief, Barda and Jasmine slid to the ground, and stood shivering in the gloom.

'This is the place,' said the dragon. 'Or very near it.'

It glanced over its shoulder, and its skin twitched. Its eyes were no longer sparkling, but dull as stones.

'There is a small village through there,' it muttered, jerking its head towards a gap between two cliffs. 'I saw it from the air. It has a wall of sticks around it. I saw humans creeping about within, like sick mice in a cage. And beyond it, I saw . . . other things.'

It shuddered.

Bess's voice seemed to whisper in Lief's mind.

There are beasts, deep in the mountains. Monsters beyond imagining. Things that crawl in the shadows. Things that growl deep below the rock . . . Shadowgate lies among them.

Lief drew his sword. He heard Barda do the same. He heard Jasmine murmur to Kree, and the clatter of wings as Kree took to the air.

The raw patches on his face stung in the icy wind. The four notes of music rang in his ears. Louder now. And again came the whisper . . .

Beware the Masked One . . .

He felt like screaming to drown out the sounds.

Will I never be free of this? he thought desperately. Did that cursed mask change me forever?

The dragon shifted its feet. 'What will you do?' it asked. Grimly, Lief noted that it had not said 'we'.

'We will go to the village,' he said. 'It is the village of Shadowgate. You can guide us from there.'

Silently Barda and Jasmine came up beside him. Together they moved towards the gap. The dragon shuffled behind them, its tail rasping on the rock, its claws scrabbling.

The gap was long and straight, and broader than it had looked from a distance. The cliffs that towered on either side of it were pitted with holes and caves. The wind howled through it like a lost soul. And they could hear other sounds—growls, scratchings and chitterings, from deep within the rock.

Here the Masked Ones came, seven years ago, Lief thought.

He could almost see the wagons rumbling through the pass, the drivers sitting rigidly, alert to every sound. He could almost see Otto, Rust, Quill, Plug, and all the rest . . . and in the lead wagon, the mammoth figure of Bess, her beloved son beside her.

Jasmine's voice broke sharply into his thoughts.

'Lief! I beg you to stop humming that tune!' she exclaimed. 'It is driving me mad! What is it?'

Lief clapped his hand over his mouth. The four notes had been ringing in his head, but he had not realised he was humming them aloud.

'It is the Happy Vale clock, I think,' he mumbled. 'It seems to be stuck in my brain.'

'This pass does not smell safe, king,' called the dragon behind him. 'And it is too narrow for me. You must find another way.'

'There *is* no other way,' Lief said. 'You will have to fly, and meet us on the other side.'

The dragon made an unhappy, gurgling sound, but spread its wings and soared upward.

'I have my doubts about that beast,' muttered Barda. 'I would not be surprised if it deserted us.'

'It is not in its own territory,' Jasmine snapped. 'Naturally it is uneasy.'

Barda hunched his shoulders and did not answer.

Lief looked up. Kree was sailing between the cliff tops, riding the wind, yellow eyes searching the ground. Above him soared the lapis-lazuli dragon, almost invisible, its underside matching the dark grey sky.

Keeping close together, glancing often behind them, Lief, Barda and Jasmine began to walk through the pass. Lief saw Jasmine frown at him, and realised that he had begun humming again. He pressed his lips together.

'That is not the Happy Vale clock chime, Lief,' Barda said. 'The Happy Vale clock went like this.'

He whistled a quite different tune, a tune with five notes instead of four.

'You are right,' Lief said, suddenly remembering. 'But then, why do I keep hearing—'

'It is probably some tune Bess taught you!' Jasmine broke in impatiently. 'What does it matter? With everything—everything else we have to think of!'

She turned her head away, biting her lips.

And at that moment, Kree screeched a warning.

Instantly the three companions drew together, back to back. There was nothing ahead of them, nothing behind. Weapons raised, they scanned the cliff walls.

Eyes glinted in every hole, every crevice. The cliff walls were alive with stealthy movement. Here, a dripping, pointed snout poked out of a tunnel. There, a bundle of blunt claws scrabbled against the rock. Bubbles of grey slime frothed silently from cracks and slid downward.

'Move on!' Barda breathed. 'On!'

They began to run. But Kree was still screeching above them, screeching warning again and again. And suddenly there was a thunderous roar that seemed to shake the rock.

The eyes in the cliff face blinked out. The snouts and claws disappeared as if they had never been.

Kree swooped downward like a black streak. The

strip of sky between the cliff tops darkened. They heard the lapis-lazuli dragon give a single, panic-stricken cry.

And then they could see it no longer, for there above them was a vast, roaring thing of glittering green, its fangs bared ferociously, its spiked tail lashing, its wings battering the air.

Lief went cold. He looked down at the Belt of Deltora. The great emerald, symbol of honour, was burning like green fire.

The emerald dragon had awoken. The emerald dragon, drawn to this place by the Belt, had discovered its land invaded by another.

'Oath-breaker!' a great voice thundered. 'Thief! Invader! Betrayer!'

Paralysed with horror, Lief saw the huge talons slashing—talons like knives—and heard the lapis-lazuli dragon scream.

'No!' he shouted at the top of his lungs. 'It is with us! It is helping us! Do not harm it!'

But his voice was drowned by the sound of the emerald dragon's fury.

'Flee, then, coward!' it roared. 'You have no honour! Turn tail like the snivelling sneak you are! You will not escape me!'

The great mass of green turned in the air and in an instant it was gone.

Suddenly there was nothing to see between the cliff tops but sullen grey cloud. They could still hear roaring, but every moment the sound grew fainter.

Barda let out his breath in a long sigh.

'The lapis-lazuli dragon will escape,' Jasmine said confidently. 'It is smaller, but it flies very fast.'

'No doubt,' Barda said grimly. 'But now they have both left us. What are we to do now?'

'We must go on alone,' said Lief doggedly.

He was trying not to think of what this meant.

The ruby dragon had uncovered the Sister of the East. Then the dragon's power had joined with the power of the Belt to destroy it.

But what would happen if he tried to face the Sister of the North alone? And how, without the dragon, would they find it?

Kree squawked urgently. Filli chattered. Lief looked up and saw that slowly the eyes were appearing in the cliff faces once more.

'Let us move on,' said Jasmine uneasily.

They ran the rest of the way to the end of the pass, and with relief burst out into the open. When they looked back, they could see that the cliff faces were crawling with movement, and bubbling with slime.

'We are well out of that,' Barda said heavily.

But Lief's stomach was churning. His knees felt weak. Cold sweat was stinging his face. His head was ringing with sound.

Slowly he sank to the ground.

'The village is ahead,' Jasmine urged, pointing to a wall visible beyond the rocks.

Lief made no answer. He feared that if he spoke he

would be sick.

He felt in his pocket for something to dry the sweat, and his fingers touched something hard. Dimly puzzled, he pulled the object out.

It was the little set of chimes Bess had given him. With it came the paper on which she had written the musical notes he was to learn, and the stub of a pencil.

Only half aware of what he was doing, Lief tapped a chime with the pencil. A soft, clear note rang out.

Yes, that is right, he thought. He tapped another note. And another. And then the second note again.

'Lief, what are you doing?' Jasmine was kneeling beside him, her face pale with strain. 'That tune again! What is it?'

Again Lief tapped out the four notes.

Music is like another language, Lewin . . . This is how we write it down.

Blankly he stared at the paper in his hand. Then, rapidly, he began to draw in the clear space at the bottom.

His pencil hovered over the paper. He glanced up at Bess's far neater writing. His face began to burn.

'What are you doing?' Jasmine repeated, frowning at the marks.

Lief shook his head. 'Nothing,' he mumbled.

This is madness, he thought. It cannot be! Quickly he turned the paper over, to conceal it.

On the other side, there was a mass of his own writing. He realised that he had used the back of Bess's lesson to write out the notices on the Happy Vale noticeboard.

With glazed eyes Lief stared at the writing. It seemed to shimmer before his eyes. Then, suddenly, letters seemed to move around, slip into new places.

And then he saw it—saw what his innermost mind had been trying to tell him for so long.

The names! The final secret of the notices was in the names. And as slowly he realised what that meant, his blood ran cold.

16 - Shadowgate

Lief met Jasmine's worried eyes. He saw Barda crouching behind her, watching him in concern. He knew he had to speak, though his head was swimming and his face and neck felt bathed in fire.

'We did not understand,' he whispered.

'Did not understand what, Lief?' Barda asked quietly, glancing at Jasmine.

They fear my mind is wandering, Lief thought.

He thrust the paper towards them.

'The names,' he said. 'They are not real names. Laughing Jack invented them.'

Jasmine's frown deepened. 'I daresay he did,' she muttered. 'No doubt his little joke amused him.'

Lief shook his head. 'Not a joke,' he said. 'A threat. A warning to Fern not to ignore—'

He swallowed. 'All these names—Dean the Smoke, Dame Henstoke, Andos the Meek, Hank Modestee, Kate

142

Mend-Shoe—are made up of the same twelve letters. Do you see?'

There was a puzzled silence as Barda and Jasmine scanned the names.

'Yes,' Barda said at last. 'It is true. "Seek the Nomad" is the same.'

'And do you remember the sign we saw on the way to the Broad River Bridge?' Jasmine exclaimed. 'Someone had scrawled upon it, calling himself "Mad Keeth Nose"—the same twelve letters again!'

'It was just after we passed that sign that Fern first spoke to us,' Lief said in a low voice. 'The sign alerted her—made her suspect who we were. The Happy Vale noticeboard told her everything else she needed to know.'

'But—' Jasmine shook her head. 'But I do not understand this! What is so special about those letters?'

Lief took a deep breath. 'Arranged correctly, they spell another name,' he said. 'The name of the guardian of the north. The name Fern spoke with her dying breath. The Masked One.'

His companions stared at him, speechless.

'But—but the Masked Ones fled!' Barda said at last. 'I saw them all, on the road to Purley. And Bess—'

Lief nodded. 'Bess is dead,' he said. 'Rust, Quill and all the rest are far away, and know nothing of this. The evil being who calls himself The Masked One—the enemy who commands Laughing Jack, as Laughing Jack once commanded Fern—is someone else.'

Slowly he turned over the paper to show the four musical notes he had written at the bottom of the page. He sang the notes one by one, as Bess had taught him. And as he sang them, he wrote down their names.

B E D E

'*Bede!*' whispered Jasmine. 'Bess's son? But—he is dead!'

Lief shook his head. 'All we know is that he disappeared into the mountains here, seven years ago, and was never found,' he said. 'So close to the Shadowlands border, who knows what evil thing he met, and what promises of power were made to him?'

'Of course!' muttered Barda. 'He was vain and spoiled, by all accounts. Once he grew tired of the poor girl he had lured away from her home, the Enemy would have found him easy prey.'

Lief gripped the paper tightly. 'The tune that makes his name has been ringing in my ears, louder and louder,' he said. 'Bess felt it too, I think. The further west she travelled, the more thoughts of Bede haunted her. Somewhere very near, Bede is singing his name, over and over again.'

'I hear nothing but the accursed wind,' growled

Barda. 'And the beasts, howling in the Shadowlands. Perhaps you hear the tune because of the Belt, Lief.'

'Or because I wore Bede's mask, if only for a little time,' Lief muttered. 'It does not matter which. What matters is that we do not need a dragon to take us to the Sister of the North. The guardian himself will guide me.'

＊

Their path took them past the walled village, but they did not knock upon the gate, and no-one challenged them. A few wisps of chimney smoke drifted over the wall, but these were the only signs of life.

'Life here was always harsh, no doubt,' Barda murmured. 'But how much worse it must be now! Surely most people have died or fled.'

Lief nodded. He wondered if the parents of Kirsten and Mariette, the two lost girls, lived on inside the wall.

What would they say if they knew that the faithless one who stole their daughters' hearts was still alive— and thriving like an evil weed within their land?

The sky grew darker as the companions began to thread through the maze of rocks and cliffs that lay beyond the village. Soon the light was so dim that they were almost feeling their way. Jasmine called Kree back to her shoulder. They lit torches, and moved on.

The clouds seemed to be pressing down upon them. Lightning flashed, and thunder rumbled ominously.

'This storm is not natural,' Jasmine breathed.

Lief stopped abruptly, and held up his torch.

'Look there!' he whispered.

A few paces ahead stood a tall stone. It looked horribly familiar.

They crept forward. Torchlight fell, flickering, on the stone.

DO NOT ENTER THIS DOMAIN!
FLEE THIS REALM OF FEAR AND PAIN!
DEATH AND TERROR BOTH AWAIT
THE WRETCH WHO ENTERS SHADOWGATE!

Jasmine shivered. Filli had scurried beneath her jacket. Kree sat motionless on her shoulder, his feathers fluffed up, his beak slightly open.

'It is like the stone that guarded Dragon's Nest,' she muttered. 'The verse seems to say that Shadowgate is beyond. Yet we passed the village long ago.'

'The village was named after the place, no doubt,' said Barda. He wiped sweat from his brow and glanced at Lief. 'Do you still hear the music?' he asked abruptly.

Lief nodded. The feeling of sickness had returned. His head was so full of sound that he could not speak. He moved past the stone, his face turned away from it.

Despair and die . . .

He heard his companions following him. I am

leading them to their deaths, he thought.

Lightning cracked across the boiling sky, lighting up the flat sheet of rock upon which they stood, and a vast mass of jagged peaks blocking the way ahead.

Lief looked down at the Belt of Deltora. The ruby and the emerald had lost their radiance, but the topaz and the lapis-lazuli were still glowing more brightly than the rest.

They shine because their dragons have awoken, Lief thought. The ruby and the emerald would shine, too, if danger and evil were not all about us. Four dragons now fly Deltoran skies. But faith and happiness are far behind us. Luck has deserted us. Honour has turned its back on us. We are alone.

'We are together,' Jasmine said loudly behind him. 'We have the Belt of Deltora to protect us. We must not fear. We must not despair.'

Lief knew that Jasmine was not talking to him. Jasmine was talking to Kree, to Filli, and to herself, defying the evil spell of the stone.

But her words cut through his haze of misery. He put his hands on the Belt. He felt the strength of the diamond, the calm of the amethyst, the hope of the opal, flow through him. He felt his mind sharpen as the topaz glowed beneath his fingertips.

And as the lightning flashed again, he saw the mass of rock ahead shimmering and changing before his eyes. He caught his breath and gripped the Belt more tightly. He watched, astounded, as rocky peaks became towers, cliffs became high, sheer walls, hollows dissolved into barred windows . . .

A vast castle lay revealed before him. Evil seemed to stream from it like a vile smell.

He heard Jasmine and Barda gasp.

'You see it,' he said huskily.

'Yes,' Barda muttered. 'Lead on!'

And Lief felt them move into place beside him.

✳

Nothing barred their way. No creature menaced them. But as they moved towards the castle door, thunder roared above them, and lightning split the writhing clouds.

'The Masked One is waiting for us inside,' Lief murmured. 'He knows we are here. He wants us to come to him.'

'So it seems,' Barda said. 'He is proud, like his evil Master in the Shadowlands. And his pride will be his downfall.'

He raised a great fist, and banged upon the door.

'Stay out here and keep watch, Kree,' Jasmine whispered. Kree squawked reluctantly, but left her shoulder and flew away into the dimness.

We have no plan, Lief thought. We are walking into the web of this sorcerer with nothing but our wits and the Belt of Deltora to aid us.

He glanced at Jasmine, and she smiled. So be it, he thought, and straightened his shoulders.

They waited in silence. They heard no footsteps.

But suddenly there was the sound of a key turning in the lock.

Slowly the door creaked open.

There stood a beautiful young woman in a long white robe.

A locket on a fragile golden chain nestled at the woman's throat. Her small feet were bare. A long, heavy braid of yellow hair, bound with golden thread, hung over one shoulder to far below her waist. Her eyes were wide and frightened.

This was the last thing the companions had expected.

Can this be Mariette? Lief thought in amazement. Can it be that she still lives? Is her love for Bede so strong that she remains with him, even now? Can it be that Bede himself . . . ?

You will quickly tire of her. Why, only last year you were dallying with her sister . . .

So Bess had said to her son. Had she been wrong?

Barda was the first to recover.

'We are travellers, caught in the storm,' he said, stepping forward. 'We beg for shelter.'

'We are not prepared for visitors,' the woman murmured rapidly. 'I fear we cannot—'

She caught sight of Lief, and gasped. Her hand flew to her throat. Then she glanced quickly behind her. Soft music had begun, drifting from somewhere within.

The woman bit her lip, and pulled the door wider. She watched silently as the companions moved inside.

Then she closed the door behind them, turning the key in the lock once more.

The entrance hall was huge—as large as the entrance hall of the palace in Del. Hundreds of candles burned in great metal rings hanging from the ceiling. Streaks of emerald gleamed in the carved rock walls.

'Follow me, if you please,' the woman said.

She turned and led them through the hall. At the far end stood two tall doors. The woman put her hands to the doors, preparing to push them open.

'Wait!' whispered Lief. 'Please tell me! What is your name? What are you doing here?'

The woman turned. Her eyes were dark with misery.

'My name is Kirsten,' she murmured. 'And I am here because once I loved too well.'

Before Lief could speak again, she pushed open the doors.

17 - The Castle

The companions moved into a vast room that was bathed in light. Its rocky walls gleamed green. Its stone floor was covered with exquisitely embroidered rugs.

A great fire blazed in a fireplace set into the wall that faced them. To the right of the fireplace was a vast table draped with a stiff, white cloth and laden with food and drink.

And in the very centre of the room, on a heap of cushions that gleamed with every colour of the rainbow, lay a young man, hung about with gold and jewels.

The man had a small harp in his hands. He was playing softly. Emeralds glittered in his ears. A circlet of emeralds crowned his shining hair. Golden chains festooned his neck and his slender wrists. Beside him lay several pens and a scattered sheaf of papers.

As the companions entered the room, the music

stopped. The man raised his head and fixed them with burning eyes.

Then Lief knew he had been right. There was no doubt that the man lounging before them was Bede.

'He does look like you, Lief!' Jasmine breathed. 'Why, you could be brothers!'

Lief did not like the thought. He stepped forward.

'Do not approach him!' Kirsten hissed behind him. 'Kneel! Kneel, I beg you!'

Her voice was so full of terror that Lief did as she asked. Barda and Jasmine hesitated, then kneeled beside him.

'What is your will, my lord?' Kirsten asked.

Bede did not look at her. 'Bring food and drink,' he said, barely moving his lips.

'Yes, my lord! Oh, but do not stop playing! Your music is so sweet!' Kirsten scurried to the table and began putting wine and fruit on a silver tray.

Bede plucked softly on the strings of the harp. Sweet music filled the room. But he did not take his eyes from his guests, and neither did he speak.

In moments Kirsten was back. She kneeled in front of Bede and put a silver goblet of wine on the floor beside the sheaf of papers.

'Ah, you have finished the words of a new song, I see!' she said. 'Is it your song for today? The one I am to copy into the book?'

Bede bent his head in a slight nod.

Timidly Kirsten picked up a paper.

'How beautiful!' she murmured, looking at it. 'Would you sing it for us, my lord? I long to hear it.'

Is she trying to distract him? Lief thought. Or is it part of her slavery that she must flatter him in the way he likes best?

His mind was teeming with questions. Kirsten was plainly in Bede's power. She was terrified of him.

But did he control her by sorcery, or by some other means?

And how had she come here at all? It was her sister, Mariette, to whom Bede had lost his heart. Where was Mariette now?

Kirsten was coming towards them, carrying the paper and the tray. Lief reached out to help her, but she shrank back, her eyes wide with warning.

'Sing, my lord!' she called over her shoulder. 'We will follow the words most carefully.'

Slowly she sank to her knees, and put down the tray. She placed the paper on the ground where they could all see it. All the time her eyes were beseeching Lief, Barda and Jasmine not to move.

There was a short pause, and then Bede began to sing. His voice was sweet and mellow as honey. The music of the harp was like the soft rippling of a stream.

Lief listened, transfixed in spite of himself. It was only when Bede finished the song, and began at once to sing it again, that he began to follow the words.

He looked down at the paper lying on the rug in front of him.

Fair as the day is my Kirsten.
Sweet as a flower she is,
Her goodness banishes evil.
She is too perfect for one such as I
A poor plain man I am,
Far, far beneath her.
But her heart is my prisoner
To me she can refuse no help,
For she adores me.

Lief glanced at Kirsten. Her eyes were swimming with tears. Her hands were tightly clasped, the knuckles white.

Only then was the spell of Bede's voice broken. Only then did Lief realise how cruel were the words sung in those honeyed tones.

He felt Jasmine and Barda shifting uneasily beside him, and knew they saw it too.

Bede was taunting Kirsten, rejoicing in his power over her. No wonder she wept, remembering a time when his singing had filled her heart with joy.

Lief felt cold with fury. Why do we kneel here? he

raged to himself. Why do we not leap on him now, and force him to take us to the Sister of the North?

But he did not move, for in his heart he knew why. The room was thick with evil and menace. Delicate as Bede chose to appear, he was plainly powerful. Very powerful.

If they were to survive, and find the Sister of the North, they had to soothe him, flatter him, make him feel safe. They had to be cunning, and stealthy. They had to play his game.

Bede at last fell silent. He raised his eyes from his harp, and looked straight at Lief. His gaze was intense and full of meaning.

Lief smiled, raised his hands and began to clap. After a moment, Barda and Jasmine joined him.

Bede did not smile. He did not move, bow or speak. When the applause at last died away, he bent his head to his harp, and began to sing the song again.

Lief bent as if to pluck a grape from the tray.

'Kirsten,' he whispered. 'Where is Mariette?'

Kirsten stiffened.

'Is she alive?' Lief breathed. 'Is she here?'

Kirsten nodded, very slightly. Her lips formed the word, 'Captive'. Her eyes were full of anguish.

And there is my answer, Lief thought, glancing at Jasmine and Barda, who were watching intently. Bede controls this woman by a mixture of sorcery and threat. She is bound to him by fear for Mariette's safety, as well as her own.

'We can help you,' Barda muttered, leaning forward as if he, too, was choosing something to eat.

'No. He is too strong.' Kirsten's voice was like a sigh. 'His power is boundless . . . terrible . . .'

Clumsily she began to pour wine. The jug clattered against the silver goblets as her hand trembled.

Lief looked over her shoulder at Bede. The man's eyes were closed. He was still singing his new song, softly, slowly, as if entranced by the beauty of his own voice.

He must feel the power of the Belt, as I feel his evil, Lief thought. He is wary of us. He is biding his time, waiting for us to let down our guard. But he does not dream that Kirsten would dare to betray him. That is our strength.

'Do you know where the source of his power lies, Kirsten?' he murmured.

Kirsten stared at him blankly.

Lief sighed inwardly and tried again. 'Is there a place in the castle that Bede visits often?' he asked. 'Somewhere you cannot follow?'

Kirsten shivered. She did not move her head, but her eyes slid sideways, towards a small arched door in a shadowy corner of the great room.

'He goes there,' she breathed. 'When he returns, he is—stronger.'

'Then that is where we must go,' Lief said. 'How can it be done?'

Kirsten shook her head hopelessly.

'There must be a way!' Lief hissed. 'Help us, Kirsten! If not for yourself, for Mariette!'

Kirsten bowed her head. Lief, Barda and Jasmine exchanged rueful glances. Bess had called Kirsten a proud beauty. She was still very beautiful, but she was proud no longer. Bede had broken her spirit.

Then Kirsten raised her head again. Her eyes were still dark with fear, but for the first time a tiny spark seemed to glimmer in their depths.

'I will try,' she murmured. She turned until she was facing Bede.

'My lord?' she called softly.

Bede's song broke off. He opened his eyes.

Lief, Barda and Jasmine saw Kirsten's back tense. They saw her raise her hand to her throat. They prayed that she would not lose her nerve.

Stiffly she gestured towards a door set in one of the side walls—the wall closest to the arched doorway.

'Your guests are tired, and wish to rest, my lord,' she said. 'May I take them to a bed chamber?'

There was a long pause.

'If that is their wish,' Bede said, without expression. He closed his eyes again, and began to strum the harp once more.

Slowly, silently, her eyes fixed upon him, Kirsten stood up and began backing towards the door that led to the bed chambers. Lief, Barda and Jasmine stood up, too, and began backing after her.

Bede's golden voice followed them.

Fair as the day is my Kirsten,
Sweet as a flower she is . . .

Kirsten glanced quickly behind her and changed direction slightly. Now, instead of backing towards the bed-chamber door, she was moving towards the arched door in the corner.

Lief's heart thudded. What a risk she was taking! At any moment Bede could open his eyes, and see . . .

But Bede's eyes remained closed. He sang on, raising his voice, as if he wanted them to hear every word of his song one last time before they left him.

Her goodness banishes evil.
She is too perfect for one such as I . . .

Lief glanced over his shoulder. Kirsten had nearly reached the arched door. A few more steps . . .

'Perhaps poems do not have to rhyme,' Jasmine whispered. 'But surely the words of a *song* should rhyme. A song like that, in any case.'

'It is no song at all,' Barda muttered. 'It sounds as if he wrote it in two minutes. Certainly he took no care in writing it down. Yet he repeats it endlessly, as though it were the best song ever sung!'

Lief heard the tiny click as Kirsten lifted the latch of the door. He felt a cold breeze on the back of his neck. Again he looked over his shoulder.

The door was opening.

Inside was darkness. And from the darkness streamed a sense of evil so strong that his stomach seemed to turn over.

Kirsten met his eyes and beckoned, urging him to make haste.

Bede's voice rose again, echoing through the great room.

A poor, plain man I am,
Far, far beneath her . . .

Barda and Jasmine are right, Bede, thought Lief in disgust. Your famous new song is very poor, and I wish I could tell you so. Bess boasted that your rhyming was perfect. But you have not even bothered to try. Every line ends with a completely different sound. 'Kirsten', 'is', 'evil', 'I', 'am', 'her' . . .

His scalp prickled. He looked back at Bede.

Bede's eyes were open. He was staring straight ahead, at the paper lying abandoned on the floor beside the tray. He was singing the final lines of his song, his voice lilting, despairing.

But her heart is my prisoner,
To me she can refuse no help,
For she adores me . . .

Lief stared. He could not believe what his mind was telling him.

Taken together, the last words of every line of Bede's song formed a message.

Kirsten is evil. I am her prisoner. Help me.

18 - The Guardian

Lief stood frozen to the spot. Suddenly, shockingly, everything had turned upside down. Images were flashing through his mind—signs that should have made him suspicious, but which he had ignored. The hasty writing on the paper. Bede's burning eyes fixed to his own. Kirsten shrinking back from his helping hand. The little arched door swinging open so smoothly at Kirsten's touch . . .

And now, from the back corner of the vast room, he could see what had not been visible to him when he kneeled in front of Bede.

The ends of the long golden chains which twined around Bede's neck and wrists were hidden beneath the cushions on which he lay. There was no doubt in Lief's mind that they led to strong steel rings fixed to the stone floor.

Nothing was as it had seemed. When he had heard

the four notes that spelled Bede's name, he had been hearing not triumphant boasting, but a desperate cry for help. Bede had been calling Bess, trying to tell her he was still alive, and needed her.

Bede was the captive. Kirsten was the gaoler. The evil in the room was not his, but hers.

Why, then, had Kirsten shown them the arched door, and opened it? For Lief knew without doubt that somewhere within that foul darkness lay the Sister of the North.

'Make haste!' Kirsten hissed from the doorway.

Lief felt Jasmine tug anxiously at his arm.

'Treachery,' he breathed. 'Be ready.'

He felt Jasmine stiffen. Her fingers tightened, then released him. She had heard.

Lief turned around to face Kirsten. She was beckoning urgently.

He moved to her side. Now that his eyes were opened, he saw how she slid quickly between the partly open door and the wall, to avoid his touch. He saw how tightly her hand gripped the doorknob.

'You first,' she whispered to him.

And suddenly Lief understood her plan. Kirsten feared the Belt of Deltora. She knew that closer to the Sister of the North she would be far more powerful. That was why she wanted him to go through the door.

Once I am in there, she will slam it after me, and lock it, Lief thought grimly. I will be trapped with the evil inside. Jasmine and Barda will be out here, unprotected. Kirsten will destroy them, and then come for me.

His mind was racing. He had to foil Kirsten's plan—take her by surprise. But she would certainly recover very quickly. She might attack them, or she might use Bede as a hostage to force them to surrender.

He had to let Bede know that his message had been understood, so that he was ready to escape.

But how? How could he communicate with Bede without alerting Kirsten?

Then, suddenly, he knew.

He turned to Jasmine. '*Ay andastand!* he said, loudly enough for Bede to hear. '*Ya wall bay frayd. Bay rady ta ran!*'

Jasmine's eyes widened in astonishment. Then, realising what he was doing, she tossed her head as if in annoyance.

'I am not afraid,' she snorted. 'You do not have to speak the language of the forest to calm me!'

Blessing her quick wits, Lief glanced at Kirsten out of the corner of his eye. Kirsten looked impatient, but not suspicious.

Suddenly he realised the room was utterly silent. The sound of the harp had stopped. Bede had heard. He was signalling, in the only way he could, that he was ready.

Kirsten raised her hand to her throat, in the gesture Lief had seen several times before. At once, the sound of the harp filled the air once more.

That is how she makes him do her will! Lief realised, with a jolt. She touches the locket hung around her neck! It is a silent threat of some sort. But what—?

A strange and horrible idea struck him. His mouth went dry. Was it possible . . .?

Whether it is, or not, I can hesitate no longer, he thought.

He put one hand on the edge of the door and ducked his head, as though he was about to enter the passageway beyond. He took a deep breath. Then, suddenly, with all his strength, he thrust back at Kirsten, slamming her against the wall.

She shrieked and stumbled forward. Lief caught her in his arms and she screamed like a wild thing as he tore the locket from her neck.

With the locket clutched in his hand he backed away from her, drawing his sword.

'Barda! Bede is chained!' he shouted. 'Free—'

Kirsten's jaws opened. She howled. And from her gaping mouth thousands of tiny winged creatures flew, swarming into Lief's face, over his neck and hands, biting and stinging, blinding him.

Lief heard Jasmine cry out, and felt her rush forward. He heard Kirsten scream in pain and fury as Jasmine's blade found its mark. He heard Barda's sword clashing against metal behind him.

Then, suddenly, the flying creatures were gone. Lief blinked and staggered, rubbing his streaming eyes. Through a haze he saw the arched doorway looming before him. Barda, Bede and Jasmine were beside him.

'Kirsten is—protected,' Jasmine was shouting. 'The dagger barely scratched her. We—'

Her eyes widened in horror.

Barda roared in warning. Bede gave a sobbing, despairing cry.

Lief spun around.

Where Kirsten had stood, a huge black figure was rising—a black-robed being whose face was a shining emerald mask. Eyes burned through the mask's eye slits. Long white fingers oozed from the sleeves of the flowing robes—fingers without nails, lengthening, clutching, reaching . . .

The Masked One.

Lief did not hesitate. He ran through the doorway, into the darkness.

✳

They stumbled along a pitch-black passageway, Barda half-carrying Bede who was hardly able to walk.

'Mariette!' Bede choked. 'Kirsten—has—Mariette.' His breath was sobbing in his throat. After years in chains, it was a miracle he had been able to get this far. Lief guessed that Barda would soon be bearing his full weight.

'Kirsten will concentrate on us for now,' Barda growled. 'Hold on to me! Keep moving!'

Lief realised that he was still clutching the locket in his hand. He shivered, and thrust it deep into his pocket.

The passage began climbing steeply upward. Stairs

carved into hard rock wound around and around in a dizzying spiral. The walls were raw, rough stone, slimy to the touch. Plainly they were climbing up through one of the castle's towers.

Echoes of their hurrying steps, their laboured breath, floated eerily from above and below. They could hear no other sound. But The Masked One was pursuing them. They could feel it. They could feel its cold menace behind them, like an icy wind.

Lief glanced behind him, as he had so often before. He saw nothing but inky darkness. No glimmer of white. No eyes burning through the gleaming mask.

It knows it can take its time, he thought. There is only one way to run. No way out. And the closer it gets to the Sister of the North, the stronger it will become. Our only chance is to destroy the Sister before it reaches us.

'The phantom—the creature of the night—was Kirsten!' Jasmine panted. 'She killed Otto. And Fern—'

'In mistake for one of us,' said Lief. 'I am sure of it. Somehow she sensed us—sent her phantom out—to destroy us. But the distance was too great. The phantom was weak—it struck out, wherever it thought we were— killed whoever it found.'

The stairway grew even steeper and more winding, and still they stumbled up, up, their legs aching, their knees trembling with the strain.

The air was thick and dead. It was faintly tinged with a sickening, musky odour that Lief had smelled before, though he could not remember where.

Filli whimpered in the darkness.

'This place smells like the City of the Rats,' Jasmine muttered.

Snake.

Lief's stomach churned. Barda gave a muffled groan.

The musky smell became stronger. The sense of evil grew. All of them were fighting for breath. And little by little they became aware of a sound—a faint, ringing sound that seemed to seep into their souls, and fill them with despair.

The song of the Sister of the North.

It seemed to Lief that the passage was growing narrower, pressing in upon them more closely with every step.

And every step was an effort. He felt weighed down. Weighed down by the heavy, musky air. Weighed down by dread.

They rounded yet another turn. The ringing sound grew louder. And there, in front of them, rose a straight, narrow tunnel, impossibly steep, with stairs that stretched like a ladder to a dim, distant point of light.

Groaning, they began to climb, heaving themselves up from one step to another, struggling towards the light. Up . . . up . . .

The patch of light grew larger. Lief realised that it was daylight. They were nearing the top of the tower.

Then Bede groaned—a terrible sound of anguished

despair. A chill ran down Lief's spine.

Gripping the step above him, he turned and looked down.

He saw Jasmine behind him. Below her, Barda was clinging to the rock one-handed, his other mighty arm gripping Bede. And below them, floating in the darkness, was an emerald mask lit by two burning eyes, and white, tube-like fingers, snaking upward.

The eyes seemed to flame. The slitted mouth hissed. The fingers seemed to stroke the walls of the tunnel.

There was a flash of brilliant light. And then it was as if the rock walls around Barda and Bede were melting, bulging into the centre of the tunnel.

'Barda!' Jasmine screamed.

Grimly, Barda began scrambling upward, heaving Bede after him. But the swollen rock was reaching out, covering Bede's legs, covering Barda's. Like vast, bubbling arms the rock enfolded their struggling bodies, greedily taking them in.

Barda raised his head. His teeth were bared, his eyes staring. 'Go on!' he roared at Lief and Jasmine. 'Go! Do not—'

And then his head was covered in a groaning, billowing mass of rock. The rock surged upward. Jasmine screamed again, kicking and struggling as it flowed over her ankles.

'Jasmine!' shouted Lief in terror. He began to scramble downward, recklessly turning to reach for her.

'No!' Jasmine shrieked. 'It is too late! Lief, go on!'

The rock had enfolded her to her waist. Desperately she pulled Filli from beneath her jacket, whispered to him, and pushed him onto the stair above her.

Wailing but obedient, Filli bounded up the stairs towards Lief and leaped onto his shoulder.

'Go,' Jasmine shouted. 'Lief, you must!'

But Lief could not leave her. And when she saw that, Jasmine lifted her hands and let herself fall back, disappearing into the mass of rock as if it were quicksand.

Lief gave a cry of anguish. Below him the groaning rock bulged and surged upward. He heard the hissing laughter of The Masked One.

A white rage such as he had never felt before boiled up within him. He flung himself back to face the stairs, looked up at the light, and climbed.

He no longer felt pain in his legs or hands or face. He no longer felt fear. He felt only that white-hot anger. It was as if it had burned everything else away. As if all that remained within him now was the will to destroy.

He reached the top of the stairs and hauled himself up into a round, stone-floored room. Only then did he look back.

Filli wailed, clinging to his shoulder. The little creature was grieving. Lief raised his hand to comfort him. He knew that was what Jasmine would have wanted. But he could barely feel Filli's fur. It was as if his fingers were numb.

He stared down into the tunnel, dry-eyed, feeling

only a vast emptiness. It was like looking down a chimney—a chimney that was now almost completely blocked, about halfway down, by a misshapen lump of rock.

The tunnel wall had been released from its enchantment. The swollen rock had shrunk back as far as it could, then hardened once more. Its surface was oddly smooth, and it gleamed like a newly-healed wound.

Through the narrow opening that remained of the tunnel, something green, black and white was oozing like slime.

Lief stepped back and looked around. The musky smell was very strong. Through small, round windows he could see storm clouds boiling around the snowy peaks of mountains. He could hear the sound of thunder, and howling wind.

But neither of these was as loud as the song of the Sister of the North, ringing from the bottom of a pit which yawned in the centre of the room.

Lief approached the pit and looked down.

The pit was writhing with snakes, hundreds of them, hissing and spitting, coiling one upon the other.

And the Sister of the North was among them. Lief could hear it. He could feel it.

Carefully he lifted Filli from his shoulder. He walked to one of the round windows and put the little creature on the sill.

'You can climb trees, Filli,' he said. 'So you can

escape from this tower. You can get down to the ground. Do you understand me?'

Filli stared at him with bright, unwinking eyes. Lief dug deep into his pocket and brought out the locket, still dangling on its broken chain.

'I want you to take this with you, and keep it safe,' he said, pressing the locket into Filli's paw. 'Keep it safe for me.'

He had no idea if the little creature understood. He had no idea if there was any point in what he was doing.

He pushed the window open. Wind howled around the tower.

He nodded at Filli. 'Go!' he said, waving his hand. 'Find Kree. Take care.'

Filli put the locket into his mouth and slipped through the window.

Lief closed it after him and walked back to the pit. He stared down at the snakes coiled within it. Rage still burned within him, but cold hopelessness had settled like ice in the pit of his stomach.

He had his sword. His arm was strong. He did not fear pain. He could kill many of the snakes, many . . .

But he would be dead before he killed them all. The Sister of the North would survive. The Masked One would live, growing in power and wickedness. Deltora would perish. Jasmine and Barda would have died in vain.

Again he looked down.

There was a slithering sound from the side of the

room. Slowly he looked around.

The Masked One was rising from the tunnel. Behind the emerald mask, its eyes glowed with triumph.

'So now I have you, king of Deltora,' it hissed. 'I have succeeded where others have failed. The Master has already rewarded me richly. Now I will have power beyond my wildest dreams.'

Lief drew his sword. 'I hope it is worth it to you, Kirsten,' he said.

'I am The Masked One,' the cold voice whispered. 'Nothing can stand against me. Soon I will bend the whole of the north to my will.'

'You are Kirsten of Shadowgate, hiding behind a mask,' spat Lief. 'And you could not bend Bede to your will. You could not make him turn from Mariette. You could not make him love you!'

Behind the cold, green shell of the mask, the eyes flashed with hatred.

The black-draped arms rose. Tube-like fingers slid forward.

They struck Lief, burning like fire. And soundlessly he fell. Down, down into the pit.

19 - The Sister of the North

I t was a nightmare. A nightmare of hissing snakes. And deep within the nightmare was evil so strong that it should have frozen Lief, mind and body.

But already he was empty of feeling. Already he was beyond fear.

He struggled to regain his feet, slashing wildly around him with his sword. Snakes thrashed around him, waist deep. He waited for the first, stinging pain that would tell him the fight was over. He wondered if it had already come, and he simply had not felt it.

The Masked One bent over the pit, the emerald mask gleaming, expressionless.

'Bede did not deserve my love!' the voice rasped. 'Seven years ago he stumbled into my castle, with my sister fainting in his arms. How he stared when he saw me, and realised whose magic had led him through the wilderness! He had his chance, then, to cast Mariette aside, and pledge himself to me. He did not take it.'

Lief could hear the snakes hissing in a frenzy, but the pressure around his waist and legs had eased.

He glanced down, and with slow surprise saw that the creatures were frantically arching their bodies away from him. Those that could were hurling themselves at the sides of the pit. They were trying to climb up the seeping walls, falling back, piling one upon the other in a tangled, squirming ring.

The Masked One had noticed nothing. Words were still tumbling through the cruel, slitted emerald mouth on gusts of panting breath.

'Even when Bede saw the wonder I had become in the year of my exile—even when I offered him a place by my side—he recoiled from me! He deserved to die.'

Part of Lief's mind heard the words. Another part was still puzzling over why the snakes were fleeing him.

Then, like a dream, the memory of another hissing, dominating voice drifted in his mind.

Remove the thing you wear under your clothes. Cast it away.

It was a memory of Reeah, the giant snake which had once guarded the City of the Rats, in the heart of Deltora.

Lief grew very still. Feeling began to return to him. He pressed his fingertips to the Belt. They tingled. And at the same time, his mind awoke.

Reeah, for all its greatness, had feared the Belt of Deltora. Especially it had feared the ruby, the antidote

173

to snake venom. How much more must these lesser snakes fear it?

And now that the ruby dragon had awoken, the gem was at its full strength. No wonder the snakes were being driven to madness!

There is still a chance, Lief thought. A chance that I can live to destroy the Sister of the North. If only . . .

He looked up at The Masked One hissing at the top of the pit. He remembered who hid behind the mask, and what he knew of her. He took a firmer grip on his sword and forced a mocking smile.

'So Bede deserved to die, Kirsten!' he said, putting all the contempt he could muster into his voice. 'Yet you kept him alive for seven years. And why? Because his voice still had power over you.'

'His songs entertained me,' said The Masked One coldly.

'Oh no, it was far more than that,' jeered Lief. 'It was because when he sang you remembered what it was to be human. You remembered how to feel. And that was what you longed for. Relief from the cold emptiness growing inside you. A chance to weep for all you had lost.'

'I—' The Masked One seemed to choke. Then suddenly it shimmered, and it was Kirsten who was leaning over the pit—Kirsten, in her white robe, her great braid of yellow hair dangling, her beautiful face twisted with rage.

'I regret nothing!' she shrieked, gripping the edge

of the pit and leaning over even further. 'I was always more beautiful, more talented, more admired, than Mariette! How *could* Bede have preferred her? How *dared* he prefer her?'

Now, Lief thought and thrust his sword upward.

He moved fast, but something else was faster. Before the point of his sword was halfway to Kirsten's white throat, a huge snake had twined around her dangling rope of yellow hair and was wriggling upward.

Kirsten screamed and tried to jerk her head back. But it was too late. Already another snake had caught hold of the braid, and another, and another.

In seconds the rope of hair was a mass of snakes writhing desperately up to freedom. The weight dragged Kirsten's head down and pinned her, screaming, to the edge of the pit.

By the time Lief staggered back, stunned and horror-struck, she had become a living lifeline. The pit was emptying as snakes in their hundreds swarmed to freedom over her head, neck and shoulders.

And as the pit emptied, Lief's strength ebbed away. He could feel it as surely as if it blood were draining from his veins.

His limbs were trembling and heavy. It was hard to keep his head upright. He could barely keep his eyes from closing. His mind was clouding.

The Sister of the North was being uncovered. Its song was growing louder. Its poison and malice were battering him like crashing waves.

Despair and die.

He forced himself to look up. Kirsten was covered in a wriggling, hissing mass of scaly flesh. And as she screamed and struggled, the panicking snakes struck at her again and again and again.

She is protected . . .

So Jasmine had said. But the snakes were striking in their hundreds. Their fangs were like needles. And with every tiny needle scratch, another drop of poison seeped into Kirsten's helpless body. She would take a long time to die.

Sickness churned in Lief's stomach. He looked down again.

There was only one snake left in the pit. And it was no snake at all. Pale and bloated, striped with thin lines of poisonous yellow, the thing thrashed mindlessly on the stinking, seeping rock.

It had no eyes. It had no tongue. It had no fangs. But evil radiated from it like heat. And from its empty, gaping mouth poured the deadly song of the Sister of the North, filling Lief's ears and his mind, forcing him to his knees.

He told himself he had to move. He had to raise his sword. He had to try to smash the thing. Destroy it. But its evil was killing him. Its song of despair and death was ringing in his ears, drowning out all other sound. With a dull clang, his sword fell from his hand.

His fingers would not move. His hands felt as if they did not belong to him. Gritting his teeth, he lifted them. They felt like heavy lumps of dough attached to his arms. Clumsily he pressed them against the Belt of Deltora.

He felt heat. Strong, beating heat. Heat far greater than he had expected. Not just in his hands, but in the Belt itself.

Confused, he looked down. His hands were shining green. A blaze of bright green was streaming between the fingers, lighting up the dark.

Dark . . . why was it dark? Lief forced his head back, looked up. The tower room was dim, as though the windows had been curtained by cloud.

He could just make out the figure of Kirsten slumped over the edge of the pit. And dimly he could see the snakes. They were fleeing, slithering off Kirsten's body and away, out of sight.

What . . .?

Lief's heart was thudding like a drum in his chest. His fingers were hot, burning hot. He tilted his head a little more. He looked higher. Up to the high, dim roof of the tower.

Then, suddenly, astoundingly, there was an ear-splitting crack—and the roof was gone.

Suddenly there was nothing above him but boiling clouds . . . and a vast, gleaming shape plunging towards him, green as the emerald glowing beneath his hands, roaring like thunder.

The emerald dragon!

The wind of the dragon's wings beat Lief down,

flattening him against the floor of the pit. Mighty talons reached for him, closed about him and lifted him into the air.

Weak as an infant, Lief rolled helplessly within the cage of the talons. All about him was open sky. The walls and roof of the tower room had been cracked away like the top of an egg, and thrown to the howling winds.

All that remained was the stone floor, Kirsten's sprawled body, and the pit.

The dragon did not speak. Its emerald eyes, burning like green fire, were fixed on the thing still thrashing in the pit.

But there was no need for words. For Lief could hear the dragon's heart beating, loud as thunder, thudding into his mind, crashing through the relentless song of the Sister of the North.

He took one hand from the emerald in the Belt of Deltora and seized one of the talons that caged him. He felt the talon's razor-sharp edge cut into his hand, felt the warm blood begin to flow. But he only tightened his grip.

And with fierce joy he saw green flame gush from the dragon's roaring jaws. He saw the vile thing at the bottom of the pit writhing in a pool of emerald fire.

Again the dragon roared, and again, till the pit was a furnace of swirling flame. The rock blackened, then began to glow.

Searing heat billowed upward. Lief cringed away from it, tried to roll himself into a ball to escape from it.

But still he gripped the dragon's talon with his left hand, and the great emerald with his right. And still the power flowed through him from one to the other. And still the dragon roared, and the pit burned.

The song of the Sister of the North rose to a cracked, piercing wail. It faltered. It stopped. A blinding flash of white light burst through the emerald flame.

There was a moment's breathless silence, as though the land was holding its breath.

Then there was a long, low groaning sound. And the next instant, the air was filled with dust—blinding dust as fine as powder, swirling in the wind. Lief screwed his eyes shut, coughing and choking.

He heard the dragon hiss, as if with satisfaction. Then he felt the wind rushing past his ears as it dropped down, straight down, to the ground.

✳

When Lief opened his eyes, he was sure that he was dreaming.

Above him, two dark shapes loomed against a background of hazy blue sky. A gentle breeze blew on his face. Someone was holding his hand.

'Lief!'

He blinked. Slowly his eyes focused and he realised that the shapes were faces. Smiling faces.

Jasmine and Barda were bending over him. Kree was perched on Jasmine's shoulder. Filli was nuzzling into her neck, his tiny paws clutching her tangled hair.

Lief stared. Now he knew he was dreaming. Tears

burned in his eyes as he waited for the vision to tremble and disappear.

But it did not.

'It was an enchantment,' Jasmine whispered, putting her arms around him. 'The spell was broken. We awoke—here.'

'And the castle was dust,' said Barda. 'Nothing but dust, blowing in the wind.' He leaned forward. 'Lief, surely this means—?'

Dizzy with joy, yet still hardly daring to believe it, Lief nodded. 'The Sister of the North is no more,' he said huskily. 'And I think Kirsten died at the same moment. It was because—the emerald dragon returned. It—'

'We saw it,' Barda said grimly. 'It dropped you onto the ground with us, then flew away. Perhaps we will see it again. But I would be more than happy not to. It had a stern, fierce eye.'

'It is the dragon of honour,' Lief muttered. 'It came to clean its land of evil, as was its duty. But I fear it is still angry, because we brought another dragon to its place.'

'It can be as angry as it wishes,' Jasmine grinned. 'It did its part, that is all that counts. It did its part, and you did yours, Lief! The Sister is gone. All Kirsten's sorcery is undone. And we are not the only ones to rejoice. Look!'

She pointed. Lief turned his head.

The castle of the Masked One had vanished.

Where its towers and turrets had risen to the sky, lay a great sheet of smooth, flat rock powdered with fine dust. Two figures stood in the centre of the rock, hand in hand. One was Bede. The other was a slender young woman with long, light brown hair.

'When the spell was broken, Mariette was freed, just as we were,' said Jasmine. 'The dust cleared, and she was standing there. She had been enchanted—imprisoned in her own locket, which Kirsten had taken for herself. But you must have known that, Lief, or why did you take the locket at all?'

The locket! Lief plunged his hand into his pocket and winced. He had forgotten that his hand was cut and bleeding. He felt around with his fingers, but the locket was not there.

'Filli has it,' Jasmine said softly. 'Do you not remember? You gave it to him for safekeeping, when you thought you would not survive. You told him to take it out of the castle. And so he did. He has been waiting to return it to you.'

'Indeed,' said Barda. 'He would not give it up to anyone else—even Mariette. The emerald dragon is not the only one in this land who values honour.'

Proudly Filli climbed down from Jasmine's shoulder, uncurled his paw and tipped the locket into Lief's waiting hand.

Lief opened the locket. Inside, as he had expected, was a small painting of Bede.

'Jasmine, your dagger?' he asked.

Jasmine passed the dagger to him. Gently, using the dagger's point, Lief prised the little picture out.

And behind it, pressed into the back of the locket, was a small pad of tightly folded paper. Lief picked it out in turn and carefully unfolded it.

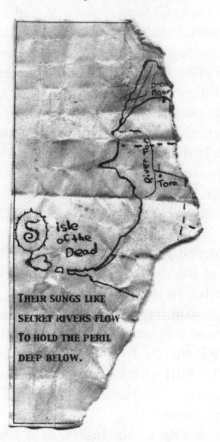

Together the companions stared at the grim name of their next goal, and noted how far away it was. They stared at the new lines of verse, wondering what they meant. But no-one said a word, and after a few moments Lief folded the paper again, and thrust it deep into his pocket.

They all knew that, all too soon, he would have to take it out again. Soon they would have to travel on, and face whatever dangers might come.

Troubling questions would have to be faced, too. How, despite all their secrecy, had the guardian of the north known where they were, almost every step of the way? Why did the Masked Ones hate the king so bitterly? Where had Laughing Jack gone? Would they see him again? Was he still a threat to them?

But this—this moment under the hazy blue sky—was not a time for plans and questions, but for rejoicing.

They were safe. The dread song of the Sister of the North had been silenced forever. At last, the land of the north could throw off its mask of death, and begin to live again.

For now, that was all that mattered.